6-15

"MAKE YOUR PLAY,"
THE KID SAID . . .

He stood away from the bar now, his right hand hovering over the low-hung holster, his face drawn and white as an actor's in the sooty light of the coal-oil chandelier. Someone coughed.

"You think on this," Cord said. "You think on how bad you really want this."

"Make your play," the kid said again.

"Bad enough for dying?" Cord persisted.

The kid blinked and his fingers crabbed for the butt of his gun, but Cord's big Peacemaker was already in his fist, and there was plenty of time before it roared in the room . . .

CORD

The Black Hills Duel

Owen Rountree

BALLANTINE BOOKS • NEW YORK

Library of Congress Catalog Card Number: 82–90868

ISBN 0–345–30758–5

Manufactured in the United States of America

First Edition: March 1983

For Kenneth P. Bangert
May 7, 1947–January 23, 1982
and
For Cinda Purdy
October 21, 1950–April 1, 1980

Chapter One

CORD JERKED THE BIG BAY GELDING BACK onto his hocks and waited until the echo of the rifle shot faded. Just ahead the canyon walls were closing together, the wagon track curving off to the left and out of sight behind a field of red-rock boulders big as haystacks. It was a bad place to be taken unawares. Then the rifle sounded again, maybe a hundred yards off, judging from the sound.

Cord drew his own Winchester from its saddle scabbard, levered a cartridge into the chamber, and eased the gelding in amid the boulders. From there he could see ahead aways. The road beyond straightened, and as Cord had figured, the canyon walls closed up tight, nearly vertical and fifty or so feet up to the rimrock on either side. There the dusty track of road was barely wide enough for two wagons to pass.

A buckboard was stopped at the most narrow point, the four-horse team snorting and blowing as though they had just been pulled up from a hard run. Cord could make out some kind of tarp-covered load on the wagon's flat rear deck. The teamster and his shotgun guard sat stiffly on the bench seat, the reins hanging slack in the teamster's hands. Behind them another seat had been rigged for two passengers. One was a man dressed all in black. He sat rigid and erect, staring straight ahead. Beside him sat a woman whose face was hidden under a gingham sunbonnet.

Five riders surrounded the wagon. Three were out front in the road, their backs to Cord, the middle one pointing a rifle up at the cloudless sky. Two others sat

1

their horses beyond the wagon, intent on the moment and oblivious to Cord.

The man with the rifle lowered the weapon so the shotgun guard could look into the muzzle and said, "Throw down that goddamned double-barrel. I ain't going to ask a third time."

The guard tossed the shotgun off the side of the wagon and sat staring at the toes of his boots.

"Now climb off there, all of you. Nice and easy."

Cord stepped his gelding out full into the roadway, held his long gun on the leader's back, and shouted: "Hold quiet, right there!"

For a long moment no one moved, except for the shotgun guard, who looked up, narrowing his eyes against the sun.

"Scabbard that rifle," Cord called. "That's the first thing. Then keep 'em high and we'll work this out."

The leader started to wheel his horse.

"Don't do it," Cord warned. "There are other guns on you."

All five of the road agents looked quickly from side to side. Then one of them pointed up at the rimrock to the left and said something to the leader.

Up there stood Chi, Cord's partner, her legs slightly apart, tall and dark and lean in her black sombrero and wool serape. Two long braids of shiny ebony hair hung almost to her waist, and her leather britches were tucked into hand-tooled boots with knee-high uppers. A Winchester held steady in her hands.

"Come around now," Cord called. "But move easy."

The leader turned his horse and stared at Cord impassively, as though this wasn't working out the way he had figured but it didn't matter all that much. He wore a close-trimmed black beard, and his face was creased and sun-darkened.

"It's this way," Cord told him. "You and your two men beside you there, you move on past the wagon and group up over there with the rest of your bunch. You keep between me and them, so I've always got a clear shot on you. You do that, and then you ride on, and there's no more trouble for anyone."

From the rimrock came the sharp clacking of Chi working the action of her rifle. The bearded man looked up at her almost curiously, then nodded at Cord.

"We'll ride," he said, "but this isn't over."

"It is for now," Cord said.

The bearded man muttered something to the man on his left and started past the buckboard. Cord let out breath. Even with the drop, two on five was short odds. He would be glad to see this unexpected facedown done and behind them.

Then Cord saw the teamster lean forward in his seat and snatch at something in the box at his feet. When he straightened there was a rifle in his hands.

Damn the fool, Cord thought, starting to bring up his Winchester.

The bearded leader reined up hard, slapped at the revolver on his hip, and shot the driver in the middle of the chest. The man flopped back onto the woman passenger, and she screamed and fought her way out from under the weight of the convulsing dying body, throwing herself into the lap of the man beside her. But he sat impassive, as if unconscious of, or unwilling to acknowledge, the violence flaring around him. He did not flinch from the gunfire, nor from the spray of blood which fell across his face in fine drops.

The shotgun guard dove from the seat and hit the ground rolling. He got his hands on the shotgun he had thrown down, then scuttled under the wagon bed. Atop the rimrock Chi's rifle barked, and one of the outlaws flipped from the saddle and landed on his back, bouncing hard and lifeless.

Then the bearded man and his pard kicked their horses quickly past the wagon, and for a single frozen moment Cord stared at the leader's back over his rifle's sight.

Then the moment broke, and Cord lowered the rifle without firing. He watched as the dust and powder smoke rose to block his sight of the four retreating horsemen. There was no profit in shooting men in the back, and Cord was anyway already beginning to regret getting involved in this fracas in the first place. He sheathed his rifle and stepped the gelding toward the wagon.

The woman seemed composed already, despite the blood of the dead teamster smeared across her dress. She untied the string under her chin and took off her sunbonnet, revealing pale blond hair and fine high-toned features. As Cord rode up she eyed him with open interest. The dead man draped over the seat beside her might not have been there.

Boots scraped on the hard-packed dirt of the road-way and the shotgun guard scrambled out from under the flatbed of the wagon. Cord looked down at him and pursed his lips in surprise. The man was about Cord's age, but there was a paunch above his belt which testi-fied to easy living in trail-head towns and nights spent dipping into buckets of beer. His boots were new and hardly broke in, and his rolled-brim Stetson had been steamed and blocked not so long before.

Cord crossed his hands on his saddle horn and said, "Howdy, Nolan. You are surely looking prosperous."

The man gave Cord a sheepish grin, then looked down at the shotgun in his hands as though he had for-gotten he was holding it and wasn't quite sure what it was for.

Cord had crossed trails with this man once or twice in the past. Mart Nolan had lived for years on the softer fringes of outlawry, working as a front man or hos-tler for a gang when they would have him around, rus-tling the odd horse or steer, even raiding some nester woman's kitchen garden when that was all he could manage. There were plenty like him in the West these days, and taken as a bunch they weren't worth a mouthful of chewed-out tobacco spittle.

"Much obliged, Mister—" Nolan brought himself up short. He at least had the sense not to speak Cord's name in front of the man and woman. Nolan fidgeted uncomfortably, then looked to the dead outlaw sprawled face up in front of the wagon, as if he was trying to figure how close he had come to not living out this day.

"Didn't see there was much I could do to help, once the shooting got started," he muttered, as if talking to the corpse. "Thought I had better lie low until the lead stopped flying. You see how it is." He looked up to Cord.

"Yeah," Cord said. "I see how it is."

Cord looked over his shoulder at the sound of a rider approaching, the quick staccato of hoofbeats in a long trot. It was Chi, her dark braids bouncing behind her. She reined beside Cord and took her time looking over the pretty blond woman, who returned her gaze steadily. Chi frowned at the man in black, still entranced beside the woman. Her frown deepened when she turned it on Nolan.

"What's he doing," she said to Cord, "showing up in this place?" She glared at Nolan, as though his paunch was an insult to her idea of character.

"Got me a job, miss," Nolan said proudly, as though he sensed nothing wrong. "Shotgun guard on the freight run. They needed an hombre who could take care of himself—and the merchandise," he added self-importantly. Nolan nodded at the man and woman. "We don't usually carry no passengers. We got more valuable property to deal on." Nolan stopped abruptly, as if he had just remembered who he was talking to and wished he'd shut up two sentences back.

"Finish it," Chi said. "What are you hauling?"

Nolan stared up at her moon-eyed, unwilling to tell the truth and too dull-witted to contrive a convincing lie. Chi snorted with disgust and impatiently rode past Nolan, up close to the wagon. The blond woman turned in her seat to follow Chi, watching her with open interest, like an explorer come upon an exotic new species. Chi stared back. She held until the blond woman

looked away, somewhat flustered. Then Chi leaned
over in the saddle and flipped back the edge of the
tarp.

Beneath were three canvas bags, each maybe half the
size of a fifty-pound sack of flour. The tops were se-
cured with leather buckles padlocked shut. Chi hefted
at one, grunting with the effort. The bag dropped to the
planks of the buckboard deck with a solid *thwack*.

"Gold?" Chi said to no one in particular, turning the
notion over in her head. But then she looked at Nolan.

The man smiled in a sickly way.

"Let's have a look." Cord drew his thin-bladed
stockman's knife from the scabbard on his belt and
tossed it to Chi. She caught it deftly by the haft and
bent to one of the bags.

"No need," Nolan said quickly. "It's gold all right."

The blond woman spoke for the first time. "Are you
planning to steal it?" she asked artlessly, her curiosity
apparently impersonal. She smiled faintly, showing
white even teeth.

Chi ignored her and turned to Nolan. It was clear he
was worrying the same question. "You tell us a story,
Little Man," Chi said.

"It come out of Virtue," Nolan said quickly. "The
gold, I mean, it come out of the camp, they call it Virtue, maybe ten miles back along the trace, and it's a
pretty rich strike, too. Mister Rawlins, he sure is going
to be pleased you two come along like you did, saving
everything and all. He'll want to shake your hand."

"Who is this Rawlins hombre?"

"Ladd Rawlins, that's his full name. This is his
freight line." Nolan prattled on, as if maybe his story
were compelling enough to distract Cord and Chi from
coming to the idea of making off with his precious
cargo. But Cord was only half listening. He regarded
the blond woman. She was maybe twenty-five, and her
long linen dress was cut just a shade tight to emphasize
the swell of her breasts above her tight-corseted waist.
Her face was very fair, almost pale, and Cord wondered
if she had the city woman's fear of sun on her skin.

"Thank you for what you did," the woman said. "We are enormously in your debt." She glanced at the man beside her, who still had not moved so far as Cord could see. "We . . . my name is Katherine Paine, and this is my husband."

"Undertaker?" Chi asked, not politely.

"A man of God." There was a hint of challenge in Katherine Paine's smile. "May I present the Reverend Zachariah Paine."

At his name the man turned his head slightly to glare out at Cord from beneath the brim of his black hat. Cord felt a sudden jolt of recollection, not for the man but for days long past. It had been years since Cord had given any thought to godly matters, but the heated intensity of the preacher's stare took him back to fervent boyhood churchgoing in east Texas, a time he had not known to still be a part of his memory.

Cord's father was a dark Germanic Lutheran, and Sundays under the hot Texas sun, sweating in whatever church-boy clothes his mother made for him, holding to his father's calloused hand on their way into the settlement and its peeling white creekside church, all that had been hell for the little boy Cord remembered as himself. For a moment, Cord could smell the gritty air and the somber sleepy horses tied at the hitch rack, and hear the whir of locusts, and see his father's anger and final sadness at the defeat his hard life had imposed upon him.

For a brief time when he was maybe thirteen, Cord had somehow come to an adolescent sense of himself as inhabited by God, to such a degree that even his father looked upon him with fear. Cord had testified before all of them there in that white-painted church, and he remembered looking out at the little congregation of thick-wristed farm people and knowing their fear of him, a boy brimming over with right-minded fervor.

Inhabited by God. That was what the preacher said. *Listen to this boy. He is inhabited by God.*

Then it passed like exorcised possession, and Cord had long since forgotten the ways religion could turn your head. But for that moment, alongside the wagon in that dusty canyon, Cord had a brilliantly disconcerting vision of the boy he had been.

"Cord," Chi said. She had been watching him with impatience touched with amusement. Cord looked over at her and knew she was thinking about the possibilities inherent in a wagonload of gold, and nothing between them but a woman, a minister, and a coward, and his mind came back to the issue at hand. If they tried it and got away clean, the gold could mean months, even years, of living any way they wanted, anywhere. Cord thought of San Francisco, and a bait of grilled oysters and bacon at one of the fine hotels.

But getting clear, anyway clear enough so there was no nagging impulse to keep checking on your backtrail, that was the part that made the notion wrongheaded. Cord and Chi had survived years of living beyond the law by careful planning, not whimsy. For one thing, this was not really their kind of job; almost since they had begun running together they had specialized in banks to the exclusion of other targets, maybe because banks were hard to feel sorry about.

Second was that Cord had learned from experience the best fighting chance came in knowing every angle. He believed in planning, escape routes, and, if possible, no shooting. This Dakota badlands territory was new country to them, but Nolan and this Rawlins character had to know it well. There was no telling what lay ahead along a trail on which they would be slowed by the weight of gold. Third, there were those four hijacking road agents, waiting around some corner nearby, feeling cheated, awaiting their chance.

That was plenty enough to make it a bad job. And Cord also had the uneasy feeling that he'd already gotten them more involved with Nolan and this blond woman and her crazy preacher husband than he should have. He frowned at the Paines, man and wife. Cord was constantly surprised at how something as simple as a daylight ride through wilderness country could so quickly turn complex.

"No," Cord said aloud. Chi shrugged and looked away.

"You riding on to Virtue?" Nolan's vast relief was evident in his tone. "Ride with us, if you've a mind. Mister Rawlins, he is sure going to thank you. Why, I'll bet he'll have some kind of reward, soon as we get there and he hears the story of what you done."

"This wagon is going to Deadwood." It was the Reverend Paine, his voice thick and deep and rich as sorghum, stating a pronouncement of the incontrovertible.

Nolan pulled himself away from the preacher's stabbing gaze. "We are like hell. This wagon ain't going nowhere but straight back to Virtue, fast as them horses can make the trip." Nolan looked pleased at himself, now that he had someone to bully around. "And I'll lay you that Mister Rawlins won't be sending it out again until he can rustle up a mess of gunhands to hold against them road agents." Nolan looked up to Cord. "It ain't going to be easy to recruit men. There's a plague of gold fever in that town."

Cord gave Chi a questioning look. She shrugged again. "We've got to provision up somewhere. Those gold camps don't usually run much to law."

"No law at all, 'cept what the miners make," Nolan said. Cord knew he was angling for two free guns to back him on the trip home.

"Just so as we don't waste a lot of time taking in the local sights," Chi said. Cord wondered if she meant this blond Paine woman or the taverns of Virtue.

"We have no need for your kind." The preacher spoke again. Nolan started to answer and thought better of it. "The mark of Cain is upon your brow, sir." Paine aimed an accusing finger at Cord, and again Cord heard the discordant ranting he'd grown up with, each Sunday in that east Texas church. It was too familiar, and jabbed at childhood anxieties like a hot needle. The preacher's eyes smouldered with devoutness, or a sort of madness Cord knew to work out to the same thing.

"The Lord said to Cain, 'And now art thou cursed

from the earth, which hath opened her mouth to receive thy brother's blood from thy hand.'" The Reverend Paine stood suddenly and shifted his accusing finger to the dead teamster slumped beside him on the wagon seat. "Genesis, chapter four, verse eleven."

Katherine Paine touched her husband lightly on his arm, and he looked down to her blankly, as if he had lost his place for the moment. Then he sat and squinted off again at nothing.

"Please excuse my husband." Katherine Paine offered Cord a sweet ironic smile. "His livelihood is the judgment of other men."

"Let's move," Chi said.

"That's the ticket," Nolan said quickly. He came around the wagon, wrestled the stiffening body of the teamster off the back seat and onto the rear platform, where it lay jumbled atop the tarp covering the sacks of gold. Blood had formed a red-black puddle on the buckboard bench, and Mrs. Paine glanced quickly at it and edged away.

"Will you leave the other soul where he lies?" the preacher demanded.

Nolan spit in the dirt a few inches from the dead outlaw's head. "If you want him, you fetch him," he muttered. But when he saw the preacher's look he stopped. "Well, what the hell?" He bent and got the other body under the arms, and awkwardly managed to hoist and twist it onto the wagon box.

"The awful beauty of the Lord's vengeance," the preacher said.

Cord and Chi rode past the wagon and on down the trail toward Virtue. Behind them Nolan was swearing at the team of four as he tried to get the wagon turned. It was near midday by now, the August sun high overhead and glaring off the rocky canyon walls. Cord pushed his dark Stetson back and wiped a sleeve across his forehead.

He glanced toward Chi in her wool serape, and realized that in all their years together he had never seen her sweat. She grinned reassuringly at him, but Cord knew she was turning over the same hunch as he: Somehow they were right on the brink of getting into more than stood out at first sight. Then Cord spotted the blue roan horse the dead hijacker had been riding, drifting and trying to graze. There, at least, was something sensible to do. Cord caught the horse and, after he pulled off the saddle, turned it loose. He piled the saddle on the back of the wagon with its former owner.

Chapter Two

THE BLACK HILLS COUNTRY OF SOUTHwestern Dakota Territory ran to rocky creek valleys sided by steep thin-timbered slopes. It was a landscape where Cord could have felt safe, at ease. From the high grassland plateaus you could see miles off over the Great Plains to the south and west, and savor the space without being out there, surrounded by the endlessness. These hills were empty and profitless unless a man found gold, but it was country where Cord could have lived, anyway for a while. It was bleak, but there was solace here as well.

The town of Virtue was simply bleak. What timber had once grown in the vicinity had been chopped from the slopes for building and firewood, and whatever brush and stumpage was left had been burned off.

Cord and Chi, riding a few hundred yards ahead of the freight wagon, topped a rise in the track and Virtue lay below them, dry and dirty and baking under the relentless high-country sun. The single street cutting through the camp was rutted dust which had once been mud. Lined on either side stood twenty or so ramshackle structures. A few, of rough-lumber wood, had high false fronts, or second-story verandas hanging at odd angles over their skewed front porches. Virtue did not look to be inhabited by carpenters. The other establishments in town were mostly canvas wall tents with hand-painted shingles hanging above the flap to signify whether the proprietor assayed gold, cut hair and pulled teeth, or served gut-scorching whiskey.

This most orderly part of town lay along the bottom of a gulch which had once been a streambed, at least in the damp season, before the upstream miners diverted all the water to sluice gold from the gravel. The hillsides above town, far as the ridges, were dotted with tents, lean-to sheds, and a few one-room cabins, all of these miners' residences interspersed with rust-colored mounds of discarded tailings and the gouged-out scars of erosion left by gully-washing spring runoff and the quick powerful fury of summer thunderstorms.

The buckboard came creaking up behind them. "There she is," Mart Nolan said proudly, as though he'd been the original town planner. "Ain't she something?"

"Yeah," Chi said. "Something to stay clear of."

Cord turned in the saddle, nodded at Katherine Paine, and touched two fingers to his hat brim. She smiled. Her husband took no notice.

"Let's see to business," Chi said.

Knots of men along the street broke off their palavering to shoot curious looks at the strangers. Someone gave a low whistle, but Chi gave no sign she'd heard. Cord was used to this sort of attention, and although it did not much suit the anonymity of a man who made his living robbing banks, a man with cash money on his head, it was a condition of life with Chi he had accepted long before. When you partnered with a high-blooded, dark-eyed, handsome Mexican woman, you knew men in camps such as this would wet their lips and make low remarks and begin to think night-thoughts. You lived with it.

Still, often as he had seen it, this staring and thumb-sucking did not sit easy with Cord. Near as he could see, Chi was the only woman in town, and these men were rough trade. By their dress—heavy dirt-encrusted denim coveralls, torn and sweat-stained cotton shirts, and limp slouch hats—every one of them was a miner. Once long ago, in the shadow of the Great Divide near Leadville, Colorado, when it was still a territory, Cord had caught a touch of the gold fever, and he knew how strong it could run. The days and nights melted into one another, and all you could think of was the pounding ache in every muscle, and washing one more pan before sundown. Most of all you lived with your bitterness, because other men, right over the next ridge lots of the time, had the luck of gold, and it was not you.

Like as not it would never be you.

Knowing that, combined with suffering the bone-wearying work, the long days of working at the stony earth, always wet with icy creek water and your own tepid sweat, such frustrations could turn men indifferent to anything beyond their own desires. Everything Cord and Chi did in this town would want a tight rein.

To their right as they rode in, alone in the center of the row of tents and shanties, one building rose two stories to dominate the street. Unlike its neighbors, it was whitewashed, a rough, smeary, lackadaisical job of painting, but white just the same. The railed balcony which ran along the second floor was square with the world and shaded a boardwalk, the only one in town. From the canopy hung a sign with red scrolled letters against the whitewashed background: "THE GILDED PALACE CASINO," and beneath, "Ladd Rawlins, Prop."

Cord looked up and down the street. From both directions men watched them so expectantly that money might have been riding on what they did next. Cord was annoyed. This caravan coming into town—a wagon loaded with two dead men, three sacks of gold, the preacher and his wife, and he and Chi leading the parade—for these men it had to be the grand diversion of the week.

To Cord's sensibility there was a scent to this town of

something gone wrong: Virtue stank of more than just
gold-rush excitement and failure. Cord could not put a
name to it just yet, but it was something to remark and
keep in mind, and cypher upon later if it became neces-
sary.

"Let's have us a drink," he said.

Chi shook her head. "There's already more trouble
today than anyone could count," she said. "There is no
sense to looking for more."

"Fine. No trouble."

"Cord," Chi said, taking it carefully, trying for some
restraint. "The less time we spend in this Virtue town
the better, any way you look at it. We can get a bottle
for riding out, if you have to have it."

"Listen," Cord said, and he was listening to himself,
"we been camped in those badlands for three days now,
and on the trail four days before that, hard riding."

"Who's fault was that?"

"I paid my ante into that pot."

"You and me both," Chi said. "Only I didn't ask to
be dealt in."

Cord scowled and looked away down the street.
There was no arguing with Chi when she was pretty
much centered in the right, and this time she had him
cold. He had screwed up, and she had paid along with
him. And she stuck anyway, as she had always done.
There was a great deal to be said for that. But she
wouldn't stand for much more pushing.

"Right now," he said, "a drink would go down real
fine."

"Cord," she said, but then she sighed and let it go.

There were times—mostly when he had been drinking and the alcohol made him lose sight of who he had
become and why he had made himself this life—times
when, it was true, he did seem to go out of his way
looking for mischief. But this was not one of those
times. Cord sat his horse in the middle of this town, and
every man in sight seemed to be challenging him to dismount. Years before he would not have stayed horse-

back for a moment, and the way he'd climb down would be like a face-slapping dare.

Maybe that had been the better way.

But now, Cord repeated, "No trouble," and turned his back on the staring men before he swung out of the saddle and looped the gelding's reins around the hitch rail in front of the whitewashed saloon. He looked up to Chi, still mounted.

"You coming along?"

Chi stared back a long time without answering. "This time," she said finally, and she came fluidly down from the saddle. "But there will be a time when I won't." Then she grinned at him and added, "Maybe." She ducked past through the swinging doors.

"Yeah," Cord said, talking to himself. "I guess I know."

The barroom of the Gilded Palace was crowded with miners. If not for the daylight streaking in through the two big front windows, it could have been midnight. Two men in white shirts and bow ties minded the long bar, in front of which were a couple of dozen round tables with battered captain's chairs drawn up. To the right there was a good-sized alcove with a roulette table, a faro case, a brightly colored wheel of fortune, and several games of *vingt-et-un*. All were getting heavy play.

Chi was not the only woman in Virtue after all. Half a dozen prostitutes were working the room. Cord watched one, a dark-skinned Indian woman with flabby sagging breasts. Her nose had been broken more than once. She took a whiskery man by the arm and steered him to a flight of stairs which led to the balcony. The whiskery man was knee-walking drunk, and halfway up the stairs he keeled over backwards and rolled down the risers like a sack of old clothes. Only a couple of men at one of the poker games noticed or bothered to laugh. The Indian whore got the man to his feet and they started up the stairs again.

Below that balcony an archway led to what looked

like a hotel lobby. Another balcony was opposite, over the gambling tables; a single door opened off it.

Although the bar was no more than planks nailed to whiskey-keg supports, some rudimentary attempts at someone's idea of elegance had been tried. A coal-oil wagon-wheel chandelier hung over the center of the cavernous two-story room, and gilded-framed paintings of plump women half hidden behind gauzy drapery decorated the back bar. In one corner stood an upright piano, painted white, at which a "perfesser" no doubt played at night.

But what Cord noticed most was the still hot air, thick with tobacco smoke and the rank odor of stale beer and body gas, flavored by the reek of unwashed men, all of it cut through by the roistering miners' raw voices. The brass spittoons scattered here and there were each surrounded by a broad circle of splattered tobacco juice.

Cord and Chi crossed to the bar, and Cord knew every man in the place was turning to study them: the tall dark gunman and the hard sensual woman in leather britches and shapeless wool serape. Some man called, deliberately loud enough to be overheard, "How would you like to drive that down to Cheyenne?"

Men guffawed lewdly. Cord stiffened. This sort of bluster, the false bravado of men in mobs, was something difficult to abide.

"Don't you even think about it," Chi said to Cord quietly. "Let's get our drinks and be done with that part of it. Then we can fetch some supplies and ride on."

Cord knew what she meant: *before the trouble starts up*.

One of the white-shirted bartenders came to them, listened and nodded, and returned with a bottle each of bourbon and tequila and two thick-bottomed shot glasses. Cord poured and downed a shot of the amber whiskey, then poured again. He could feel the burning warmth of the peppery liquor settling into his gut, and he sipped more slowly at the second shot. After a long moment of consideration, he said abruptly, "That's just the way it is. Some things have a way of sticking in my craw."

"You settle yourself," Chi said. "The last thing we need is your acting up."

Cord finished the whiskey and poured a third shot. He stared down into its oily slickness and did not respond.

"Goddamn you, Cord," Chi said, without much heat. "Hasn't there been enough hell for your taste lately?"

Cord turned the glass slowly between his thumb and forefinger. He knew what she was referring to, and she had the right. Still . . .

"I don't know," Cord said. "I guess maybe not."

Chi had wanted to give Cheyenne a wide berth. The railroad had been through for a good ten years now, and Cheyenne was turning into a city. Chi and Cord never had much luck in cities. More people meant more law, and better law—anyway tougher law. The odds of someone matching their faces with the wanted posters were too high, Chi pointed out, and the banks were older and stronger and better guarded against the likes of them, with time-lock vaults and such.

But Cord had reasons that favored riding in. They had been drifting since they left the Owyhee River country of northern Nevada. They crossed north of the Great Salt Lake Desert, skirting through the mostly open prairie south of Pocatello, Idaho, because they had had trouble up that way not so long before. Then they holed up alongside Bear Lake, in the northern part of that vast stretch the Mormons had long since staked out as their promised land, camping and fishing for a week before dropping over into Wyoming. There they spent two days in Green River, getting a last taste of town living before drifting south into Colorado and along the lower reaches of the great Rockies, the white peaks standing sentinel to the south all the time. Cheyenne was another four days, so that by the time they rode over the last crest of sagebrush hillslope, following along close to the Union Pacific Railroad tracks, they had been wandering in the country most of three weeks.

That had been one reason for riding in: Cord wanted a drink and the company of other men. Then they were low on money, and had no prospects in sight or mind. Cord argued they couldn't pass up any chance to look over the possibilities. Besides, in all his years on the trails, Cord had never been in Cheyenne. He had trailed cattle nearby once, on a drive to the hi-line country in Montana Territory—that was way back in his youngster drover days—but he had never been in the town itself.

None of those reasons stood too strong on its own, and even taken together they didn't make up a real persuasive case. But then, Cord was restless and Chi was becoming fractious, which she got when cash money and ideas were coming slow. So what the hell, Cord decided. Just for a day or so, things were going to go the way he said, and no wrangling over it.

The saloon in Cheyenne was on Second Street, down by the railroad stockyards. It wasn't much more than a low-roofed shack, with a board-and-trestle bar and two tables which didn't match. The customers fit right in with the slummy decor. There were railroad men in striped coveralls and billed caps, with forearms like Smithfield hams and barrel chests built to solid muscle from switching track and wrestling couplings. They were mixed in with a few of the stockhands who worked for the yards, sallow, mean-faced men too continually worthless and drunken to hold work out on the cattle ranches, forced to live in squatters' shacks by the tracks and breathe coal smoke instead of country air.

Just inside the door Chi put her hand on Cord's forearm and said, "You sure you got to have these drinks?" She had a fair notion of what was coming next.

"That's right," Cord said. "I'm sure."

Cord looked around the room, going from one face to the next, as if he could stare down the crowd. The men stared back, hooded eyes flicking from him to the striking woman at his side. Cord showed them all a broad grin. There would not be much difficulty finding what he sought in this company.

But the thought brought him up short for a moment as he took his place at the bar. What he sought was trouble, and this was clear to him as it had never been before. Sure as hell, men changed as they put on years. Maybe they got worse, and that was not a pretty idea. Cord shook his head. He'd deal with himself tomorrow.

"Let's get it done with," Chi said.

The bartender was a stocky middle-aged man who looked as though he had gotten too agey for railroad work. He put both hands flat on the bar and said, "No ladies allowed."

"Bourbon whiskey and tequila," Cord said. "Two glasses and leave the bottles." He showed the bartender his finest challenging smile. The man studied Cord a moment, and saw in this grinning stranger a reminder that his own best fighting days were long behind him. He shrugged and went to fetch the liquor.

Cord had some drinks, and by and by he started to feel fine. Whiskey was dependable, always worked the same; that was what made it hard to put behind him for long. After two shots he would feel the warmth spreading up from his gut into his head, and he would know he was going to be entire and complete within himself for a while.

Three shots, and he was awash with crystalline lucidity, seeing his past and understanding it, all his life straight out behind him and large and still and simple, a wide trail he had followed and would continue to ride, and for good and purely logical reason.

His life was like stories, to ponder and fit together into a history. Cord stood poised, the whiskey glass in his hand, deep in himself and this his fifth shot, and that was when the black man came in.

Cord sensed his presence before he saw him, a strong quick big man walking light, and when Cord turned he saw a for-real cowhand, the hard calluses and rope burns on the thick lighter palms of his hands, and the turned-under and tapered heels of his riding boots. The black man wore a clean woolen shirt and serge britches, and when he took off his buff Stetson Cord saw he had straightened his hair and slicked it back with some kind of greasy dressing. It was a Saturday night, after all. This man would be in off one of the big ranches out in the hill country, and this the only place that would serve him drink.

"Hey there, friend," Cord said easily. "What's your name?"

"Name is Flint." The man's voice had a deep edge to it, and little trace of the drawl Cord had expected. "And I ain't your friend."

Cord's grin went broad as the Missouri. "Take a drink with me, Mister Flint," he said casually.

The black man eased down the bar and took Cord's bottle of bourbon by the neck. Cord was aware that the other half dozen men in the room were watching all of this with slack-jawed anticipation, like children hearing a favorite story they knew by heart.

"I'll take a drink," Flint said, "if you tell me one thing."

"Sure."

Flint upended the bottle, and air bubbles rippled through the liquor. Two inches of bourbon were gone when he put the bottle down.

"What's a good-looking dark gal like her"—he gestured with the bottle toward Chi—"doing with an ugly white son of a bitch like you?"

Cord looked over his shoulder at Chi. She was staring straight down into her shot glass, knowing there was no stopping things now, and nothing to say which would be to the point.

"You ever have any real dark meat, sugarcake?" Flint spoke over Cord's shoulder. "You feel like showing the boys here what you'd do with a real man."

Chi gave no sign she heard.

"You got any objections to me using your gal to show the boys a trick or two?" Flint demanded of Cord.

Cord cupped his shot glass in his left hand.

"Well," he said. "Yes."

"Well," Flint aped. "Maybe I don't give a good god-damn . . ."

Cord whipped his left hand around and caught the man in the middle of his dark face, just at the bridge of the nose. The shot glass inside Cord's fist shattered and he felt broken glass cutting into his palm, but he also heard the satisfying loud crack of the black man's nose breaking.

Flint took a step backwards and sat down hard on the floor. Blood gushed from his nose in a heavy stream.

Chi had taken a few steps away. Cord grinned at her, but the gaze she returned was utterly expressionless.

Then Flint was on his feet again and closing on Cord. The black man came around with a lunging right, but Cord stepped inside the blow and hit him twice in the stomach, then caught him on the point of the chin. Flint tried to butt Cord in the face and Cord danced back—but not quite quickly enough. The hard top of the black man's greasy head caught him on the shoulder with enough force to send a hard blot of pain through it, as if something had broken.

At the far end of the bar someone blew a shrill whis-tle three times.

Cord went back off balance and Flint's huge fist caught him on the point of his jaw. The punch rocked Cord's head, but the black man left himself open, and Cord got in two hard jabs to the kidneys and a clubbed fist to the temple. Flint had lost a lot of blood by now and he was starting to slow. His big shiny head was down, and his eyes were dull and glassy. Huge drops of his thick red blood plopped to the floor.

Then, suddenly, Cord saw it ending, pictured himself pounding his fists into the other man's face until Flint was sprawled out in the filth on the floor, snorting and bubbling, and the image soured the whiskey in Cord's stomach. He put both hands on Flint's shoulders and pushed hard. Flint bounced over a chair and it splin-tered under his weight as he went down. Before he had stopped twitching, Cord was on his hands and knees, puking out an acid gutful of curdled bourbon.

He was trying to get back to his feet when something cracked across the back of his skull. Brilliant flashes of light burst before his eyes and he went down again, but not completely out.

Hands under his arms lifted him, and a young clean-shaven face drifted into focus. Below the face was the blue uniform of a city policeman. So, Cord thought fuzzily, jail. Some times it came to that.

The night air outside brought him around some. "No tricks now," the cop said, "or I'll have to use my billy club again." There was a nervous tremor in his voice, as if he had not been in this line of work for long. "That nigger Flint is a bad 'un," he went on, like he was trying to make friends. "But he rides for Mister Martin, and Mister Martin don't like us to . . ."

The unsteady voice and the supporting hands fell away and Cord came down in the alley darkness beside the body of the young cop. Before he had time to cypher on that, Chi's voice was in his ear. "Goddamn you, Cord, you walk. You get up right now and you walk, or I'll leave you where you lie, swear to God on it."

Cord did not remember much about the rest of that night. Somehow with Chi's help he got to his feet and made it horseback. When the gray dawn broke he came aware of himself on the vast treeless high plains of eastern Wyoming. He'd been out in the saddle most of the night. His head was pulsing with sharp spasms of pain from the beating and the whiskey as well, and his left hand, where he held the shot glass, was stiff and puffy and criss-crossed with cuts. It would be useless for days to come. At least he'd had the sense to not swing with his gunhand. When you began to forget that sort of caution, even if drunk, it was time to give up the whiskey, or figure on being dead.

Chi was cantering along a ways ahead of him, and Cord thumped the gelding in the ribs and rode to catch up, heading into the rising sun. When he came alongside she looked at him with neither pity nor anger, and nodded as if satisfied he was in more or less one piece for another time.

Chi did not have much to say about his carrying-on in the railroad bar. Cord knew she wouldn't; there were things he did that she hated at the time, but she did not hold them against him later, like a score on some grudge tally. If Cord could work out a path through life that bypassed that sort of craziness she would have been happier, he knew. But she at least understood that sometimes it had to be this way for him and she would not use his bad spells as a weapon.

So when she did speak, all she said was, "He didn't even know who you were."

Cord blinked at her. "That Flint?" His tongue felt thick and swollen as his head.

"The *policia*." She surprised him by suddenly laughing. "When he saw you and the black he near to wet himself. I don't think he was much more than twenty, a *muchacho*." She looked up at Cord and grinned. "But *muy simpatico*. I didn't hit him very hard."

This was anyway an improvement, Cord thought. He recalled how coming back into the open space of wilderness always did wonders for Chi's spirits. Despite the aches and pains, he was feeling better himself. The edge of the sun had climbed above the flat horizon now, and the day would be clear and cloudless and plenty hot enough.

"Fine," Cord said. "We're away?"

"No," Chi said. "Not just yet."

She turned in the saddle and Cord followed her eyes. Far back across the grassy plains, at least three miles off, a puff of dust hung in the air and he could make out the vague images of mounted men. Maybe the young cop hadn't recognized them, but someone else in that bar had put together the drunken fistfighter and the hard-bitten woman in the serape and come up with Cord and Chi, the bank robbers—and worth ten thousand dollars each, dead or alive, anywhere. Cord watched the posse for a moment, then turned and scanned the country ahead, figuring timing and chances.

There was no question but that they would run. One of the rules was that you did not trade bullets with lawmen, because that was a fight you could never win. If you happened to kill one, even if he was just some town marshal, every other man with a star tended to take it real personal, and after that there was no peace for you no matter where you went.

There was also little concern that they would not get clear. Cord's bay gelding and Chi's big mare were bred for speed and stamina, and they had been cared for. It was an old habit, ingrained in Cord ever since his trail-driving days: take care of your animal first, then see to your own food and drink.

It was not a sentimental notion. In the borderless expanses of the West a good horse in strong condition was the primary tool, much more than transport, the main help you had for getting your work done. For riders like Cord and Chi their horses were survival, even more than their guns.

And Cord and Chi had plenty of practice in outrunning other riders; it came with the territory they had staked out. They had this edge as well: the chase only took them nearer to wherever they would end up next, but it took the men in pursuit mile after mile farther away from homecooking and a roof and a wife-warmed bed.

So some of those riders down there had to be thinking twice. Cord and Chi had reputations with their guns, if ever they were treed. On the other hand, the idea of twenty thousand dollars' worth of rewards could block out desire for the usual comforts and fill men with forced courage.

In the end Cord and Chi got shed of the good citizens of Cheyenne, but it took nearly three days of hard riding before they finally foxed the posse in the badlands south of the Black Hills. They made a cold camp that night, but the next morning, after Cord had scouted through the surrounding hills enough to satisfy himself they were clear, they brewed coffee. Later, as they moved up into the scrub timber country, Cord brought down a white-tailed deer. After another three days, when the monotony of a coffee-and-venison diet was starting to tell, they agreed it was safe to move out of hiding, at least so far as it took to provision up.

Now, standing at the bar of the Gilded Palace Casino, Cord told himself Chi was right, and it was time he stopped locking horns with her. He would put the whiskey and the reckless trouble-making and all that went with it behind him—*at least for a while*, he compromised in his mind—and begin looking at prospects. She accepted a lot from him, but she demanded a good deal in return. That was the fair bargain they made, and when he stopped holding up his end it was all over. Right there was a notion Cord did not care to consider.

Trouble was, this trip had already gone way beyond simple. Breaking up that holdup, that was the kind of involvement Cord and Chi spent a lifetime avoiding. Running into Nolan and recognition just made it worse.

"Okay," Cord said. "Let's finish up and ride on."

"Bueno." Chi tossed back what was left of her tequila. Cord put down his glass, still half filled, but as he turned he found himself toe to toe with another man, a slim-waisted dandy wearing a tailored coat and matching trousers, and a boiled white shirt with a ruffled front beneath a four-in-hand tie. He was hatless and his dark hair was pomaded.

"State your business," Cord said. Over the man's shoulders he could see miners eyeing them.

"I'm Ladd Rawlins. They tell me your name is Cord."

They, Cord thought; *and just who the hell were "they."* But he said nothing. Too often, men knowing his name was the prelude to trouble.

"I'd like to buy you a drink, talk to you," Rawlins said. He glanced around the room.

"We were just on the road," Chi said.

"Upstairs. I own this place."

"Good for you."

Rawlins smiled politely at her. "You did me a good turn, so I owe you. Give me a chance to make good on it."

Chi looked at Cord. Like her, there was nothing about this he liked much, but they both knew no one ever profited by turning away from information or opportunities. Chi tossed her head impatiently and looked away.

"Come on," Cord said to her. "We're already knee-high into this. We might as well see how much deeper it gets."

Chapter Three

LADD RAWLINS'S OFFICE WAS SOMEWHAT like his saloon: Whatever attempt had been made to gussy it up had more or less missed the mark. The rolltop desk set against one wall was crafted of hand-worked oak, but the finish was chipped and scarred with cigarette burns and scuffs from the shoes of the clerks in whatever express office it had spent its early years. Beside it stood a small safe. The spiral-pattern oval carpet was worn and dirt was ground into the thin nap; the pictures on the walls were of the same school as the ones downstairs in the saloon, except the women wore more clothing. Over the desk hung a calendar from "The Galvanized Hardware Company, Akron, Ohio." It featured a lithograph of two miners by a creekbed, one holding a big shallow-sided pan, the other a long-handled spade.

Rawlins sat in a wooden swivel chair as beat-up as the desk. At the other side of the window fronting the outside balcony was another chair, this one covered with crushed velvet, with several tears from which tufts of kapok were trying to escape. The man sitting in it looked up with amusement as Cord and Chi came into the office, like a theatergoer who had just heard the first notes of the overture. He was maybe forty, short and stocky and somewhat soft-looking, and he wore a soiled white shirt buttoned to the neck, without necktie or collar. Over that he wore a linen vest. Baggy britches, high-top shoes, and a narrow-brimmed derby hat completed his costume. Cord could feel the heat in the look Chi gave this hombre. There were some men who rankled her from the git-go.

"Drink?" Rawlins gestured at an unmarked decanter atop the desk.

"No," Cord said.

"I'll have one," the man in the derby hat said.

Rawlins looked at him abstractedly. "Help yourself." The man in the derby strolled to the desk and splashed a couple of fingers of whiskey into a glass. He half raised it in the direction of Chi and Cord in sardonic salute before knocking it back. He refilled the glass before he returned to his chair, balancing it on his leg while he dug a cigar out of his vest pocket and lit up.

"I'm obliged to you," Rawlins said, ignoring the man with the cigar. "Nolan told me what happened."

Mart Nolan came into the room as though he had been called, and stood in one corner, leaning back against the wall. Chi shot him a glance. Nolan met it for a moment, then dug out a penknife, worried free a blade, and went to work picking at his fingernails. From the looks of them the job was long overdue.

"That's not all Nolan told you," Chi said, still watching the big man in the corner. "He also put a name to us."

"That's right," Rawlins said tonelessly.

"Nolan," Chi said, "has a goddamn big mouth."

Nolan pushed off from the wall. "You don't scare me, lady." But he was muttering to his fingernails. "Not now that I'm back in town. You better remember I got friends here."

"You keep shooting your mouth off, and you're going to need more than friends. You'll need eyes in the back of your head."

"There is boys in town who could figure uses for you."

"Yeah," Chi said, "there's uses for you too. Like food for the hogs."

The man in the derby laughed.

"That's enough, Nolan," Rawlins cut in. "You get downstairs and have yourself a drink." Nolan folded the knife and sidled toward the door. "And you make sure you keep clammed up tight, like the lady says."

Nolan went out without answering or looking at any of them. Shouts and laughter and the clinking of glass came louder into the room before the door shut behind him.

"Sure you won't have a drink?" Rawlins asked.

Cord fished makings from his shirt pocket, but Chi plucked the tobacco pouch from his fingers. She tapped the rough-cut into the creased brown papers and used her teeth to pull the drawstring tight again. Two wrinkled smokes took shape between her tapered fingers. She struck a lucifer on the seat of her leather britches, lit both, then handed one to Cord.

The man in the derby watched this ritual with interest.

"You've got nothing to be afraid of in Virtue," Rawlins said.

Cord blew out smoke. "That sets my mind to ease."

"What I mean," Rawlins said, "is that there is no law here, except the miners' court. And all they are concerned with is short-weighing, claim-jumping, and some general in-camp thievery."

"But then," the man with the derby hat put in casually, in a whiskey-thick gravelly voice, "there's also that dead-or-alive money on you two. Twenty thousand dollars is what I hear. That's federal money, now that robbing those banks, even out here in the territories, is a crime against the crown, so to speak. Federal money is a sure thing to collect, everyone knows that. Some of the boys would take an interest in you if they knew all that." It was a long speech, and he spoke it with care, sounding sure of himself.

Chi dropped her cigarette and ground it out under her bootheel before moving across the room, her Spanish spurs making melodious metallic sounds. Both her hands were hidden under her serape.

"That kind of talk," she said, "can get people killed."

The man in the derby hat gave Chi a broad smile.

Chi's right hand came out into the open. She held her long-barreled Colt Peacemaker in front of the man's face, the muzzle pointed at the ceiling, so one practiced flick of the wrist would track the weapon down into the man's face. His smile melted away.

"Who is this hombre?" Chi demanded.

"This is Maxwell Prentiss," Rawlins said. "He's got nothing to do with any of this."

"That's right," Chi said. "You tell him to remember that." She lowered her revolver slowly and slipped it under the folds of her serape, then abruptly turned away.

"I didn't need Mart Nolan to tell me who you two are," Prentiss said to her back. "I knew soon as you rode in ahead of the wagon. It's a big country, but how many men partner up with a woman—'specially one who looks like you?" Prentiss drained the whiskey from his glass and eased to the desk for a refill. "It's my business to know that sort of thing."

"Exactly what is your business?" Cord said.

Prentiss looked happy. He had been waiting for someone to ask. "I'm a writer."

"Say what?"

"I am a romancer, a storyteller of the great West."

"Prentiss writes dime novels for Beadle and Adams," Rawlins explained. "He's on a trip around the West gathering material. Some years ago we were . . . you might say . . . associated, on a kind of a business deal, so when he heard I was in Virtue he came to look me up. He'll be moving on."

"Right now would be soon enough for me," Chi said.

But Cord was staring curiously at the man in the derby. Cord had seen dime novels, of course, cheap rough-paper books with lurid woodcuts on the covers, supposed to tell all about the true adventure of people like Cody and Hickok, Wes Hardin and Jane Canary and the rest of those famous names, and having about as much to do with real life as horseshit had to do with apple pie. But Cord had never stopped to think about who made up such fairy tales. It came to him now, looking at Prentiss, that it could hardly be fit work for a man.

"Prentiss won't be talking you up," Rawlins said, "and neither will I. I make my living as a gambler, and you only survive in that business if you play by the rules. That means you make sure not to get caught if you cheat, and you don't sell out a man who has done you a good turn."

"That's swell," Cord said. "Now that we've got that settled, let's talk some real business."

Rawlins nodded. "That freight wagon you bailed out belongs to me. It only runs as far as Deadwood—from there the Wells Fargo line goes down to Cheyenne—but it's the only way to ship gold out of Virtue, unless a man wants to chance it by himself. Not many do. It's a rugged and dangerous ride, and besides, no one wants to spend that much time away from his diggings."

"Gold is something of a preoccupation hereabouts," Prentiss put in.

"There's been talk of hijackers spotted up in the hills for maybe two weeks now, but that kind of rumor is part of any gold camp. That ambush you broke up this morning was the first actual attack. Nolan said you killed one man out of five."

"That's right."

"Four to worry about," Rawlins said, half to himself.

"Could be more," Cord said. "They might decide to take on other boys before they try again."

"I mean to stop them before they have the chance,"

Rawlins said. "I'm offering you two a job. I want those road agents out of my mind."

This would take some figuring. It was in their line of work, in a general way of speaking, but it was not Cord's prime choice of occupations. There was something to it that didn't ring exactly straight and true. Not that such things ever did, but this one definitely looked more skewed than usual. Rawlins's story made sense as far as it went, but there looked to be some parts missing.

"You know what I'm thinking, Ladd?" It was the novel writer, Prentiss, speaking as though he had forgotten Cord and Chi was present. "We could use these two in other ways."

Cord stared at the stocky man, slightly nonplussed by his brass. There was something half sideways about him, as if some of the realities of life were eluding him. Or maybe he thought himself exempt from them: He wasn't even carrying any visible weapon.

"What are you talking about?" Rawlins asked, a little sharply.

"Options."

Chi was about to say something. "We'll ponder on it," Cord cut in. "Let's get out of here," he said to Chi.

"Wait a minute." Rawlins crouched in front of the safe, blocking them out with his body as he twirled the dial. The latch handle made a metallic grating sound when he twisted it, and the hinges squealed. From inside Rawlins took a bulky brown paper envelope.

"There was near one hundred thousand dollars in dust and nuggets on that wagon." Rawlins straightened and rifled through the envelope's contents.

"I've got to have better help than Nolan," he said. "That is purely evident. And I believe in paying for my protection."

Rawlins fanned out five crisp one-thousand-dollar bills like a winning poker hand.

"For services rendered. You're not obliging yourself. But understand: This is how I pay."

"You remember," Chi said. "No obligations." The money disappeared under her serape.

"There are rooms for you in the hotel. You'll want some rest."

Cord said nothing, but there was little to this business he liked. He felt he was being hazed into a chute he had not chosen.

Outside the office, standing on the balcony, he paused to look down on the milling crowd of miners in the saloon below.

"There's plenty gnawing on you," Chi observed.

"Five thousand dollars is a lot of money."

"Maybe too much."

"Yeah," Cord said. "That's what's gnawing on me."

Chapter Four

"LOOK THERE," CHI SAID.

Near the end of the long bar, across from where they were standing on the balcony, Mart Nolan was talking with his head bent close to the man beside him. Cord was pretty sure the man had not been in the Gilded Palace when they climbed the stairs with Rawlins. Unlike the miners, the man wore trail clothes, and his revolver hung low on his hip in a tied-down holster.

Nolan nodded his head toward the balcony, but when he glanced in that direction and saw Cord and Chi watching him, he looked quickly away. The other man took his time, straightening and turning to face them full before tipping back his hat to look them over, his movements deliberate and stylized, and right out of that hard gunman way of acting Cord had seen men put on so often, and lately found so tiresome. The man's face was smoothly clean-shaven, and he was younger than most of those around him.

"Let's get the horses to the livery stable," Chi said. "They'll be wanting grain."

"Not just yet."

"What we don't need right now is another hullabaloo."

The young man was still looking up to them. He touched two fingers to his hatbrim, the salute as exaggerated as his other gestures. Then he turned away slightly, stepped away from the bar, and suddenly drew his six-gun and dropped to a crouch, scanning the room with the pistol and his foolish grin. Men stared at him warily, unsure what he was about.

"Near fast as my brother," the man said in a loud voice which carried in the silence he had created. He rose from his crouch. "Maybe faster. Guess we'll have a chance to see, when he rides in."

The young man flipped the revolver around in a road agent's spin and tipped it back into his holster, glancing up at Cord again, looking pleased with himself. Cord shook his head at this show-off tomfoolery.

"There is a boy who is like a snake ready to strike," Cord said to Chi. "The way I read this, there is going to be a row sooner or later. Maybe we can pass it by, but if we can't, I would rather see it coming than have it edge up on my blind side."

"Let's just get out of here," Chi said.

"For now," Cord agreed.

The noise in the bar had picked up again, and the young gunman was back to conferring with Nolan. Chi and Cord were halfway down the staircase when Nolan stood and called over to them.

"You all going somewhere already?"

The room quieted again.

"Gunfighter!" the young man called. "My pard here is talking to you."

Cord and Chi stopped at the bottom of the stairs. The quiet was almost absolute now, down to the scuffling of boots and the buzzing of flies. The ratchet clack of the wheel of fortune in the gambling alcove slowed its tempo and then stopped.

"You see a way to pass this one by now?" Chi asked quietly.

"Probably not."

"Do what you have to." She stepped away from him, down off the last step of the staircase.

Closer up, Cord saw the loud-mouthed gunslinger was just out of the house, eighteen at the outside. So few years, Cord thought, and so many grandly foolish notions.

"He's not your pard," Cord said to the kid. He did not have to raise his voice in the room's stillness. "Now you pay attention. I'm moving on out of here. No trouble unless you've got to have some." Even now Cord held to the idea there might be a way of talking around the nearly inevitable and deadly conclusion toward which they were edging.

Men were shuffling backwards from the bar and away from the line of fire. Others jostled for the best spot from which to witness the action. Cord watched Mart Nolan step away from the kid, grinning slack-jawed at this mischief of his making. Cord realized Nolan had drunk quite a bit in the brief time since Rawlins had kicked him out of the office upstairs. Maybe he was always halfways drunk.

"You want to back down, gunfighter?" the kid called. "See you don't trip over your tail on the way out."

A few miners laughed. Cord ignored them. He heard someone coming down the stairs behind him, but paid no mind to that either. Chi would be covering his back. But from the edge of his vision he saw Maxwell Prentiss slip by and ease along into the crowd, grinning in anticipation of the show which had to be coming.

"What's chewing at you?" Cord asked the kid, careful to keep any tone of challenge from his voice. This was it, he thought, his last concession at trying to turn all this aside. "There's nothing been done to get you steamed."

"You say." The kid snorted contemptuously, but now he also saw that this had gone beyond the point of turning, and he could not keep his voice fully clear of nervousness. "A man like you," he went on, "who has got himself a name and the repute that comes with it, another man don't need a reason to call him out." The kid managed a sneer. "So that's what I'm doing, calling you out."

There was no sense to this; there never was in this kind of showdown. Cord knew there were men who believed in some sort of gunfighter magic, some wonderful quickness of hand that would make up for everything the world ever denied.

Once, years before in Abilene, Kansas, Cord had encountered a shootist named J.W. Baron. In those days Cord believed in the magic himself. He thought he could take it from this Baron and have it for his own, and that then he would live forever and never have trouble with spooks in the night.

It had not taken Cord long to learn that it worked the other way. Now J.W. Baron was dead, though not from Cord's hand, and Cord had lived to learn that there was no magic at all in gunhand sureness. Pistolry had to do with the willingness and strength of mind to stand there while another man shot too quickly, and take your own careful time and shoot to kill. You had to be fast, sure, but more important you had to be able to transmit death with that one first shot, without hesitation or regret. You did not need to worry about the chance to show off your lethal skills. The opportunity would come again and again as long as you lived, because you would always be crossing trails with men puffed up with addled notions of *pistolero* sorcery.

To Cord, this confrontation in the Gilded Palace was mindless as a dogfight.

"Make your play," the kid said.

He stood away from the bar now, his right hand hovering over the low-hung holster, his face drawn and white as an actor's in the sooty light of the coal-oil chandelier. Someone coughed.

"You think on this," Cord said. "You think on how bad you really want this."

"Make your play," the kid said again.

"Bad enough for dying?" Cord persisted.

The kid blinked and his fingers crabbed for the butt of his gun, but Cord's big Peacemaker was already in his fist, and there was plenty of time before it roared in the room. The kid died before his own gun was clear of its holster, the heavy .45 slug catching him in the center of his chest, flattening and mushrooming as it cored through the resistance of muscle and organ and bone. The impact spun the kid around and he caromed off the bar in a reeling backwards collapse before he crashed to the floorboards.

The willingness to kill: Keep that in your mind before anything else when it starts, and do not flinch from it. Cord put his back to the bar and covered the room, searching men's eyes for the predisposition to trouble. Chi stood a couple of steps up the stairs, her Colt drawn and backing his play. Every man stared back and none moved. Wispy strands of black powder smoke hung nearly immobile in the still rank air.

Dark blood began to spread in a rough circle under the crumpled body of the kid, but the faces Cord stared at for those long moments remained blank of shock or pity or anything else that transmitted human emotion. Cord stood alone in the center of this static impassive company, and wondered what in hell had brought him to this unlikely day.

Chapter Five

THE BOY SET THE PLATES ON THE TABLE and said, "Ten dollars, mister." Cord dug in his vest pocket and pulled out a thin sheaf of currency. He peeled off a five and counted out five ones, handed them to the boys.

"Ten dollars a plate, mister. Them are beefsteaks."

Cord looked at the boy. "That must have been one prosperous cow."

"I reckon," the boy said solemnly. "They trail them all the way from Wyoming." The boy didn't look much older than eight, and scrawny for his age. He wore a once-white apron stained with grease and gravy, its hem trailing almost to the floor.

Cord shuffled through the bills. There were four dollars left. Chi handed over one of Rawlins's thousand-dollar bills and the boy took it without apparent surprise and gave back the other currency. "Getcha your change," he said and went back toward the kitchen.

Cord speared a chunk of fried potato and chewed it gingerly. It tasted of rancid lard. He pushed the spuds to one side of his plate and sawed off a piece of the meat. It was some better, and although he wasn't feeling that much appetite, he put his mind to finishing it off.

No one had tried to stop them from walking out of the saloon after the gunplay, and no one had bothered them since. It had been a fair fight, if there was anything fair about a boy like that trying to go against a man who had spent a lifetime living by his gun. The

facedown had left Cord touched by melancholy; it set in
his mind the image of the gun-happy young man he had
briefly been, and the knowledge of how easy killing, or
death, came to such boys in this country. That one in
the Gilded Palace had died for something that did not
exist. There was no shootist conjury, and the world was
changing.

Chi sensed his mood and did not try to draw him out
of it. Their career together was supposed to be simple
and unencumbered, but more often these days the
twists and ravelings of their trail led to intricate in-
volvements, their sense elusive as truth. Maybe it was
the reputation they carried like unwanted saddle bag-
gage, bringing more trouble than glory. Maybe the
years had soured the taste of the owlhoot life. Cord put
that last thought out of his mind and gave over his concentration to attacking his stringy beefsteak.

When there was nothing left but the bone and a rind
of fat, Cord pushed the plate away and asked the boy
for coffee. No woman would come to this town to tote
victuals in a café, not when there were pokes of gold to
be made catering to the miners' baser hungers. And any
male older than the scrawny child in the filthy apron
would be out in the goldfields, up to his elbows in the
chill water of the creek, swirling the heavy pan for the
telltale sparkle of color that heralded a placer of gold.
Cord wondered what had brought the boy to a place
like this, who his people were and what they thought of
bringing up a kid in a place where everything—society
and status and the everyday homebody life that defined
normal communities—everything was ruled by the fever for gold.

The miners in camps such as this drew mostly Cord's
contempt; he did not like what he recognized in them
because it touched on a raw nerve. Panning for a strike
of gold and the holdup business had things in common,
when all was said. The freedom of the life of the gun
was something you had to take, and it did not come
without a struggle, just as gold suffered a man to wrest
it from the earth.

Cord turned his mind from the circle of these ideas.

Chi used two fingers to fish the makings from Cord's shirt pocket, and built two cigarettes. *"Que piensas?"* she said, after the cigarettes were lighted. "Ride on, or stick it out?"

Cord shook his head. He was coming to the same question.

Common sense said ride on, and right now, with the money and away from more trouble. Too many things in this miners' camp of Virtue did not cypher. Rawlins and the way he had of riding a wide loop around the full facts, and the writer-man, Prentiss, acting like everything around him was a melodrama staged for his especial edification and beguilement. The dead kid in the saloon, looking for some niche in a heroic world only he could see from the enormity of his inexperience—and finding a quick and final lesson about mortality instead. Cord did not even know his name.

And that shirt-wipe Nolan, nosing around the fringes with his jaw all the time flapping away, like secrets were burning holes in his brain. Nolan was a debt. The kid was dead because of Nolan.

Nolan had one coming.

"We're in pretty thick already," Cord said carefully from behind a cloud of cigarette smoke.

That right there was the part that went against the urge to head on up the trail. Once you got tied in you had to see it through; that was how you played out the frolic of your life. You did not let yourself be chased away, neither by someone else nor by your own apprehensions. By the lights of the life he and Chi had been all these years inventing, that was the way of it. If you did not stick you were nothing but a saddle tramp, and truly no different than these rock-busting mining-camp losers.

You would come to moving on because you were afraid of what would catch up if you did not, and that would be a defeat beyond imagination.

Money and guns would never fight the real spooks— the ones you carried with you the moment you took to running. Once the fight was entered the only defense was to stand your ground and face it off.

Much as you could, leave a clean track on your pride.

And there was the idea of Nolan. Nolan was another good reason to stay.

"Something tells me," Chi said, "that it's going to get a whole degree thicker before it's over."

"You got a hunch?" On the important things that might go bad if instinct got garbled, Cord had learned to trust Chi's sense of the future.

She pursed her lips. "More like reckoning it out. There's plenty of tricks going on in this town, we know that, but up to now we haven't gotten a look at the whole picture. We need to know more."

"Yeah, and I guess we'll stick until we do."

"I guess we will," Chi said.

But she was no longer looking at him. Cord turned to see Maxwell Prentiss come into the café. He moved over to their table and said, "Mind if I join you?" and pulled out a chair without waiting for an answer, turning it around and straddling it, his arms folded on the back and a fat cigar in the fork of his fingers.

"What do you want?" Chi demanded.

"Coffee." Prentiss snapped his fingers in the air and the boy came over with the pot and another cup. When he had finished pouring, he dug into the pocket of his apron and dropped a double handful of wrinkled bills in front of Chi.

"Thought it had skipped your mind," Chi said lightly.

"No ma'am," the boy said soberly. "You got to have a good memory to do waitering."

Prentiss smiled down at the money. "Spending your ill-gotten gains?"

"What's that supposed to mean?"

"Nothing. It's just a writerly way of saying. Like 'pound of flesh.'"

"You're talking yourself into a hole."

"Money," Prentiss said. He puffed blue cigar smoke

across the table. "In Virtue it means very little. Gold is the currency of this town, the currency and the life-blood. You see how the men are in this town—they live for nothing else. Did you observe how they watched you in the saloon, Cord, when you were setting up to kill your young antagonist? It was a few passing moments of entertainment, like a music-hall turn. Nothing is real for them but the gold." Prentiss was warming to his topic. He threw out his left hand palm up and struck a pose. " 'See, sons, what things you are! How quickly nature falls into revolt when gold becomes her object!' "

"More writerly ways?" Cord asked wryly.

"Shakespeare," Prentiss said, puffed with pride as if he'd written it himself. "Henry the Fourth, Part Two. And the old boy was right. Gold, when it is found in such concentrations as we have here, seems to become imbued with power. It takes on worth beyond that of its equivalence in currency. It embodies magic and arcane strength. Men come to believe that possession of gold can give them possession of its mystical powers as well."

Again Cord thought of the childish superstitions of the kid in the saloon, and how they had brought him to death.

"Of course the whole concept is warped," Prentiss went on, "and so too, Q.E.D., this is a town shaped by a malevolent misconception. The values of every citizen of Virtue—values social, moral, financial, religious, cultural—all are shaped and distorted by gold. You've already got an inkling of where it all leads."

"No kidding," Cord said. "Now what's this got to do with us?"

Prentiss parked his cigar in his mouth and rubbed his palms briskly together. "I thought you might like to know which way the wind is blowing." Prentiss leaned forward confidentially. "You know, if this all works out, it will make for a smashing story."

"If what works out?" Chi said. "What kind of story?"

Prentiss pretended not to hear the question. "There

are three kinds of men in Virtue," he said, "so far as gold goes. A few have struck it rich—the original strike is almost two years in the past now—and are sticking around because they spent the fortune soon as they found it. Most of the others are still looking for their first real color. Every man among them is certain to-morrow is his big day. The rest get hold of their gold without digging for it. There are very few of them."

"And one is Ladd Rawlins."

"Of course. A few smart men got out with money from the first strike; a few more smart men are taking their money out of the town. My old friend Ladd is quite the savvy businessman. He simply supplies that for which there is the greatest market demand—liquor, gambling, and whores. He does real handsomely at it."

Prentiss slurped up the last dregs of his coffee and snapped his fingers for more. He was enjoying the attention. Cord figured that had a lot to do with his choice of profession. Being a writer was probably something like being an actor, so far as the need for notice and the urge to show off went. As a last resort men made up lies and passed them off as truths. It was a thing Cord saw constantly in barrooms.

"Ladd started out on the Mississippi," Prentiss said. "I met him on the paddlewheeler *Sultana*. He was seventeen years old and shilling a faro bank run by George Devol. Before he was twenty Ladd had his own card room on the *Annie Laurie*."

"If he's such a fine-handed gambling man," Chi said, "what's he doing in this mudhole town?"

"There was some trouble . . . in Denver."

"Or somewhere," Cord said. "There's always trouble for that kind."

"A man deserves his chance to recoup."

"Sure. And Rawlins' kind always does it with other men's money."

Prentiss tipped his chair back. "There's one thing you can't take away from him: Ladd can judge a man. In his line of work you get sharp at that. He figured how he could use you people right off."

"For what?"

"For what he said." Now Prentiss was all innocence. "You know about the road agents—firsthand. Anyway, that's your kind of rough-house business, not his." Prentiss's smile had twisted into a smirk.

"What about you, Mister Fancy Man?" Chi demanded. "What are you doing in this gold town? There's sure no dirt under your fingernails."

"Nor heavy dust in my poke, ma'am."

"So what does this have to do with you?"

"I told you. I am simply an historian of your wild and lawless frontier."

Prentiss hiked himself up and dug in his back pocket and came up with a dog-eared book. He tossed it on the table and Cord took it up. It was a thumbed-over copy of issue #768 of *Beadle and Adams' Dime Library*. Above a lurid woodcut of a leather-clad hombre twisted around to fire his rifle from an impossible position atop a galloping pinto pony was the title: *Buckskin Frank Leslie, Dead-Eye Defender of the Prairie; Or, The Scout's Savage Vengeance*. The author was "Colonel Maxwell Prentiss."

"Colonel?" Cord asked.

"An honorary title."

Prentiss's cigar was down to a thumb-sized stub. He dropped it into his coffee cup and it went out with a sour-smelling hiss. Cord stared at the man with horrible fascination. What, he wanted to know, did any of these fabrications have to do with life?

"There is a story in the two of you," Prentiss said. "I could weave myth from your lives, smooth and easy as Ladd can cut an ace."

Cord found the idea instantly appalling. He could learn to live with people telling lies about him. That came with having your likeness hanging on the stone walls of sheriffs' offices all through the territories. So far as Cord knew, he and Chi were still wanted for an express-company job in Virginia City, Nevada. Cord knew for a fact the job had been the work of John Mack Savage and six boys from out of the Sacramento

Valley; he and Chi had been holed up on a fishing stream outside Taos in New Mexico Territory at the time. But he'd never bothered to make a point of it. Such strange misinformation just came and went. After the first few times, you were wanted for everything.

Then there was the outright taradiddle. A story had gone around a few years before to the effect that nearly all the money Cord took went to his widowed mother in Philadelphia—and his true mother dead and ten years buried outside San Antonio. There was nothing a man could do about such crap, but to encourage the deliberate contrivance and dissemination of such stories about yourself, written down to thrill wet-eared schoolboys in Boston and thin-armed clerks in Wall Street—that struck Cord as sucking up to the most vile and rank pig-swill inflation of yourself.

Chi ground her cigarette butt angrily into her plate. "Don't you even think about it," she said to Prentiss, her voice rich with loathing. "Don't you consider for one moment turning any part of my life into your trashy stories."

Prentiss's smile dimmed and the light in his eyes went a little stale, so Cord saw the taint of defeat in them. Cord imagined the dime novelist traveling the West, sampling one man's life here and another's someplace else, twisting them around so they came out barely recognizable, and all the while never living any life of his own. Trying to get others to play out his fantastical dreams and dramas, all the while oblivious to any kind of rightness or consistency with the real world.

But Cord kept his counsel on that. Little as he respected the romancer, Cord saw how the nosy bastard could be used. There were things he and Chi had to know, quick as possible. Cord could already scent more of what had dogged them since sunup, violence coming at them from strange angles.

"That boy in the saloon," Cord said. "Who was he?"

"The one you gunned down?"

"Mister," Chi breathed. "Your mouth takes some awful chances for you."

"You got nothing to worry about, lady," Prentiss said quickly. "Nor do you, Cord. It's like Rawlins said. That boy rode into town no more than a half hour before you did, coming from the east. The business between you and him, far as the miners are concerned, it was just some fine entertainment for livelying up a dull afternoon. It was according to Hoyle, man to man."

Prentiss looked around the little café. Now he had the attention of a half dozen other men digging into the greasy overpriced grub. The more people were listening, the finer he talked, like provisioning up on words came dear to him.

"There's no one in town who will side up against you, far as gunning that boy goes." Prentiss raised his voice. "Ain't that the truth, boys?" Men's heads dipped back to their plates. Prentiss dropped his voice to a more intimate level. "At least not yet," he added.

"I never liked asking the same question twice," Cord said, just as quietly. "With you, Prentiss, it won't happen again. Now you tell me: Who was that boy?"

"Nobody," Prentiss said. "A kid, riding into a town, blowing about his brother . . ."

"His brother," Chi repeated to herself.

". . . his brother, and his blazing gun hand, but really just another kid saddlebum, and no faster than any ranch baby you ever saw practicing fast draws down by the creek, with a cloth holster sewed by his mother and a six-gun carved from a plank of yellow pine."

"What did he want with me?" Cord said.

"He wanted your hair. You are the Samson, Cord, the first he'd ever met, with the strength to bring down the temple. The boy wanted to steal that strength, to be known the length and breadth of this great land—by taking that strength upon himself."

"Say what you mean," Chi ordered.

"There's stories about you, whole lifetimes of stories," Prentiss rolled on. "Tales of Cord, the iron-willed bank robber, the deadly shootist with the quick-draw fast as a scorpion's strike, celebrated and feared from

Old Mexico to the high plains of Montana, from the muddy Mississippi to the rugged Pacific coast . . ."

Prentiss made an exaggerated gesture out of tipping his derby to Chi. ". . . and you also. Miss Chi—the dark woman, whose exotic demeanor makes men who've looked upon your beauty draw away from their wives in the darkness of night and drift into unreachable fantasies. Lovely as a nymph is the lady Chi, they say, and quick and venomous as the diamond back rattlesnake." ·

"Which kind of horseshit?" Cord blurted incredulously. "Lies like that could . . . answer my question: What did that kid want? He had to know he was courting trouble."

"The stories," Prentiss said. "He wanted the stories to be about himself. Don't you think?"

"This kid," Cord said. "Did he have a name?"

Prentiss was very pleased. This was the question he had been awaiting.

"Danny Culhane. That's what Mart Nolan called him."

"Culhane," Chi repeated, rolling the Irish of it on her tongue.

"Does that name ring a familiar note?" Prentiss needled. "Have you ever met a man with just that same name?"

They waited for him to go on.

"If you have not, today will be your day."

Prentiss made a show of pulling his timepiece from a vest pocket and snapping open the dented brass cover. "An hour or maybe two, I'd say." Prentiss clicked the watch shut. "That will be a thing to see."

"You keep talking," Chi said. "You cut a straight trail to the end of this story."

She could be pushed too far, Cord knew, especially by men like this Prentiss, and then . . . she had taken an instant dislike to the dreamy self-centered writer. Cord smiled to himself as he watched Prentiss. The man was tethered on a short rope, and even if he didn't know it, it was getting shorter.

Right then Prentiss made a mistake. Instead of answering Chi he said, "Wouldn't that be a story to tell:
Cord and Culhane, the two most notorious shootists in
all the territories, facing each other down in the middle
of a dusty Dakota street. See it: The sun is pounding
down like fire and not a man in the crowd dares take a
breath. Both men draw, faster than it can be told, but
only one stands to live out the moment."

Prentiss was on a stampede now, not even fully
aware that they were still there before him and that he
had talked lots more than was strictly healthy. He drew
a breath to go on.

Chi's hand whipped out from beneath the table and
cracked across Prentiss's face, so hard the writer's head
snapped back.

"It was you who set it up," Chi hissed. "You knew
the *muchacho* was Culhane's kid brother. Nolan sicced
him on my partner here, but you were the pig bastard
who put the idea into Nolan's head in the first place,
even knowing all the deadly twists it would lead to. You
did it, didn't you?"

"You can't prove . . ."

Chi backhanded another vicious slap across Prentiss's face, so both his cheeks burned blood-red.

"Weren't you?" Chi said again.

Chi was probably right, Cord figured, and mad
enough so this could go to guns. That would not be the
play against an unarmed man, even a belly-crawler like
Prentiss.

"I would not say another word if I were you," Cord
cut in, staring at the writer. "She gets this way, and
there's not a thing anybody can do. She is dead set on
stopping your story-mongering, and you won't like the
way it works. She does it with a mean streak."

Prentiss's face was twisted into a pasty grimace of
white-edged fear. The storyteller was peeking into the
window of real life.

"From here on, " Cord said, "you keep your fairy
tales to yourself. We don't figure in any of them. You
understand?"

Prentiss nodded, looking near to fainting.

"Now you had best leave us alone. Move easy. It doesn't take much to put the lady right beyond herself at this point. You keep that in mind the next time you see her."

Prentiss made an effort to recover his sardonic grin. "You aren't going to come gunning for me, are you, sweetheart?"

"Sweetheart?"

This time Chi used her fist, hardly rising out of her chair, but the blow hard enough to knock Prentiss over backwards. He landed on his butt and pulled the chair down atop himself. Someone across the room guffawed.

Chi was standing, her hands still empty of weapons. "Speak to me," she said softly. "Say something about how you are sorry. Do it, you son of a bitch. You got no pride and this is proof of it. I'm going to walk on you like you were floor."

"Okay, lady," Prentiss moaned.

"Are you sorry?"

Prentiss had made it to his hands and knees, looking up to Chi like a fat hound dog. "Okay, lady, I'm sorry."

"You sure are," Chi said. "The sorriest son of a bitch I ever saw." The thinnest of smiles was on her lips.

"Get out of here." Her voice was near a whisper.

Prentiss dragged himself sideways and scrambled out the door.

Chi sat down again, stared at Prentiss's overturned chair for a long time. Finally she turned back to Cord.

"Culhane," she said reflectively.

"Yeah," Cord said. "Coming here." His eyes narrowed. "What does that mean to us?"

"More of the same," Chi said. "Trouble."

Chapter Six

TWO MEN ON HORSEBACK RACED DOWN the center of the hard-packed street, each lying flat on the neck of his horse, each lashing viciously at his animal's flank. Dust threaded up behind them and drifted in through the open batwing doors of the saloon and through the pinned-back flaps of the wall tent emporiums, coating the already filthy clothing of the miners who stood in knots, cheering the contest. Dust was a fine white powder over everything.

At the far end of the street, each rider jerked up hard enough to set his mount up on its haunches. Each man snapped the reins to one side, yanking the horses' heads around, and then they had wheeled and were galloping back down the street. The leader, a big roan, was maybe half a length in front when a forefoot caught in one of the wagonwheel ruts frozen in the sun-baked mud, and the crack of the bone breaking was like a gunshot.

The animal twisted and buckled and pitched forward onto its neck, the momentum carrying him over in a great awkward flailing somersault. White bone showed through the broken foreleg. The rider catapulted out of the saddle and arched through the air before slamming into the hard-packed gumbo clay a good twenty feet beyond the place where his horse was writhing.

To the men gathered along the street sides, gripping steins of beer or holding whiskey bottles by the neck, this was fine entertainment. The downed rider tried to push himself up and let out a ghoulish scream of pain.

He clawed at the right sleeve of his red cotton shirt, ripped it up finally to reveal a glistening greasy shard of bone stabbing through the bicep muscle and skin, blood darker than his shirt welling up around it.

A fine justice, Cord thought, looking down from the second floor of the hotel. The horse would be shot, and the man would lose his arm to the fracture. Cord imagined the man going through life with the limp right sleeve folded and pinned up to his useless empty shoulder socket, hanging back in barrooms, forever excused from labor, and pitied by all who came upon him.

While Cord watched, one of the spectators crossed to the horse and stood staring down with his revolver in his hand, waiting or praying for nothing Cord could fathom, maybe just enjoying the sight. The other men were turning back toward the taverns again, and other games of chance.

The man with the revolver went on watching the floundering horse. Cord raised the window before him and drew his Colt from its holster. He dropped to one knee, rested his right forearm on the windowsill, cupped the wrist in his left hand, and sighted in carefully on the long horse-killing shot. When he fired, the man below jumped back as if it were he who had been hit. The horse shuddered, its feet drawing graceful arcs in the dust, and then came the final seizure and the quick dying fibrillations. The man with the revolver looked up whitely at Cord in the window and scuttled quickly away, apparently afraid he would be next.

Cord stood and closed the window against the dust. Below on the street, the man with the broken arm regained his feet, staggering and woozy from shock and pain and loss of blood, and no doubt from booze as well. Where he had fallen the sun and wind had already mostly dried the blood to a darkish stain. No one moved to help him as he wobbled away. In this town of Virtue, a man weakened or injured was no use to anybody.

Somebody should shoot that man like the horse he'd crippled, and Cord's Colt was still in his hand as he thought this. So he holstered it and turned away from the window. The hotel room housed a narrow iron bedframe with a thin mattress laid across iron bands, a chipped sideboard on which sat a chamber pot and a coal-oil lamp, and a single straight-back chair like the ones in the saloon below. This was Chi's room, at the far end of the second-floor hallway, and as soon as they had come in she had curled up on top of the threadbare blanket, facing the wall and drawing her serape around her.

Now, at the sound of the gunshot just outside her window, she raised her head and looked over her shoulder at Cord. But when she saw him close by, and he nodded his head that it was nothing to be concerned about, she turned away again and was immediately back asleep.

Cord listened to the even rise and fall of her breathing. In his sort of life, solitary and set apart from the pursuits of other men, there had to be some person besides yourself to care about, and for him that person was Chi. This always seemed like a new discovery when he thought about it. Cord knew how important it was to have someone around, someone you could stand. Ending up alone and crippled on the streets, talking crazily to the wind and begging from other men, that was only an accident away. Like the man with the busted arm, he thought, seeing again how the others down there had turned their backs. Cord did not want to end his days in that rowboat.

Chi's fine features, the high cheekbones and the delicately sculpted nose and dark even brow had relaxed in sleep. She seemed somehow softer, hinting at gentleness Cord sensed in her but seldom saw. Cord reached out a hand and brushed the back of his knuckles along her cheek very softly, barely touching skin to skin, but close enough to feel her warmth and the caress of her exhalation.

This partnering with a woman was a strange and tricky business. Through all their travels they had stayed away from the temptation of sleeping together, sensing it would cripple them and their thinking in some crisis—somebody would add love into an equation which called for cold logic, and they would die for it. But the affection and draw of body was always there—to be resisted.

She could sleep anywhere, any time, and Cord envied her that. Since childhood he had never been able to nap when the sun was up. Even at night he found his slumbers interrupted too often by vague dreams fleetingly remembered. There would be the sudden awareness that his eyes were open in the darkness, and then he was full awake and trying to see something that was never there. He would lie still and wait for whatever was coming next, and that would not do either. Mostly Cord hated sleeping inside other men's walls. He was generally all right outside, where he could see the stars or at least some weather crossing the moon, on those times when he awoke in the night.

After what seemed a long while, Cord took his hand away from Chi's cheek, and sometime after that he went out, closing the door gently behind him, walking softly.

Down on the street, two men on horseback had gotten ropes around the front legs of the dead horse and were slowly dragging the carcass off to the magpies and scavenger dogs. Men were shouting instructions and encouragement. But when Cord came out on the boardwalk which fronted the hotel and casino, they stopped their roistering to stare at him, gaping like children at the zoo. One group of maybe a dozen, across the street and off a little to Cord's left, stood in front of a plank shanty with an Indian blanket draped over the doorway. A hand-painted sign dangling above the door read "SALOON" with the "S" painted backwards. Mart Nolan was at the center of this cluster, and one of the men with him pointed at Cord and elbowed Nolan in the ribs.

A little farther down, in front of a wall tent marked "LAUNDRY," two men had picked the only mudhole in town for a fistfight that was degenerating into a wrestling match. One of the men had fifty pounds and six inches on the other, but the smaller man got onto the big man's back and rode him down into the muck, using all his weight to smash the big man's face into the depth of sloppy water. When the small man got off finally, the big man did not move.

Then, at the far west end of the street, with the burned- and timbered-off hills in the background, Cord saw a buckboard pulled crossways to block the way. The team had been unhitched and the wagon tongue was flopped in the dirt. Miners were moving toward it, hollering for others to come along. Cord made out two people climbing up to the buckboard's flat cargo deck.

It was the Reverend and Katherine Paine—a tall scarecrow man in a black suit and hat, and the blond woman, the passengers who had been on the hijacked freight wagon when this sour-tasting day got started.

The sun was hanging fire at two o'clock in the afternoon haze, even hotter than it had been when they rode in. The sky fairly crackled with the brilliance of its blue, without a trace of cloud anywhere, and the air absolutely still. Cord breathed through his mouth and could taste the flavor of the alkaline dust suspended in it.

Though the miners gathering down toward the end of the street didn't seem to realize it, this was a day when both men and horses should have been shaded up. Cord had shaved himself in his hotel room, and now he could feel the sting of sweat in his pores. He should have found a barber and let him slap on some bay rum. Even if Chi did hate the smell.

Cord walked along in the street and melted into the fringes of the crowd, which now numbered well over a hundred miners. Men glanced at him, but the real show was on the parked buckboard, and no one spoke to him or made an issue of the presence of a notorious gunfighter.

The preacher wore a flat-brimmed black hat with a high rounded crown, a black frock coat with skirts hanging nearly to the knee, and black woolen britches tucked into unadorned black boots. His thick black eyebrows scowled down over dark hidden eyes, and his sideburns were long and curled, like those of a Jewish merchant in San Francisco. For a man of God there was something sinister and passionate, something almost pagan, to the man.

Katherine, standing beside him, was his utter opposite, looking pale and studiously angelic. Her thick wavy hair, lustrous as electrum in the merciless sunlight, hung loose around her shoulders, and Cord realized it was years since he had seen a woman with her hair down and unadorned outside of a bedroom. She wore a billowing white gown with its hem down to the buckboard's plank flooring, thin enough so a man could see the faintest outline of her legs and hips underneath. The gown was cut in a deep low arc in front; the tops of her breasts and the valley between glistened with sweat.

The Reverend Paine extended his right arm full length, his forefinger extended, and swept the crowd with it. *"Heed my words, unworthy sinners, or eternal damnation is surely your only true destiny."*

This came roaring out in an extraordinary tone, a speaking voice which sent a deep rich basso reverberating from the surrounding hills. Cord felt the tremor of it in his gut like an involuntary shudder. It cut through the murmuring of the crowd like a sword, and men looked up, curious and moved despite themselves.

"This unfortunately christened town of Virtue," Paine boomed, "is a Godless Gomorrah, and you, its citizens, are bounden servants of the Arch-Fiend. Fall to your knees, you sinners, and beg the Lord's forgiveness, for if you do not repent your beastly vileness, you will be condemned for all of time to come."

"Sing it, preacher!" some man called, and that triggered a chorus of catcalls. As a diversion, this was even more unique than a horse race or a saloon gun-down. Cord saw that Paine had a way and a talent with these men, and they recognized it.

"The Book of Romans warns us," the preacher shouted, "that 'the wages of sin is death, but the gift of

God is eternal life.' Which would you have? Would you have a life of foulness and corruption, abomination and vice, and then a forever of unspeakable suffering? Or would you have a life of piety and cleanliness, of strength and goodness, and a hereafter of heavenly bliss? Answer me on this!"

"Make mine whiskey," a voice called from the crowd.

"Vice," another man hollered. "That's my idea of heavenly bliss."

"These are the lists of your unpardonable transgressions," Paine intoned in his heavy ringing voice. "Gluttony, for strong drink and the pleasures of the flesh."

"Amen!" The cry came from a miner near Cord.

Paine went on, unheeding. "Avarice, for material wealth and debasing gold."

"Amen!" another called.

The preacher drew himself straight and glared around.

"You who desire the riches of the earth only to enrich yourselves, heed the words of Matthew and know that no man can have two masters. 'Ye cannot serve God and mammon.'"

"Amen, amen!" Others took up the refrain.

"Sloth, because your frantic search for the noxious yellow metal is the most wicked laziness. You abandon your home and fields, and your helpmates and your manly vocations, and you answer to the siren song of gold."

"AMEN!" The mob of miners shouted out the benediction in raucous unison. If Paine's objective was to rivet their attention, he was doing a hell of a job.

But Cord, standing back at the edge of the crowd, was watching Katherine Paine. She stood with her head lowered modestly, as if in penance or from shame, her hands clasped before her and her expression sweetly blank. Cord wondered what part in all this explosion of emotionality she was supposed to play. Then the preacher went into his windup, and Cord got a hint of the answer.

"And there is lust," Paine ranted. "Lust for Eve personified: woman, the root of every other flagrant impiety, the mockery of man's ultimate weakness."

Paine turned to his wife and laid one of his heavy dark hands on her bare shoulder. "Look thee upon the true face of Satan's greatest tool, every man's ticket-of-passage to hellfire and Pandemonium."

Katherine stood still as if she were moonstruck.

"Pandemonium!" The preacher boomed out the word again, and his fingers kneaded at his wife's shoulder.

She was his prop, Cord saw. Near as he could figure, Paine was aiming to combat lust in his audience by arousing it in them.

"Look upon this irredeemable harlot, the devil's instrument of man's destruction. The Lord God said unto Adam, 'Because thou hast hearkened unto the voice of thy wife, cursed is the ground for thy sake; in sorrow shalt thou eat of it all the days of thy life.' "

The crowd was seething.

"I'll eat some of that," a man shouted.

"Amen, brother."

"I got lust for you, sister, if you need a try."

Still Katherine did not move. She seemed curiously untouched by her husband's harangue or the miners' lewd calls, as if there was nothing in this she had not long since learned to tolerate.

Yet even if this were part of a well-rehearsed act they had performed in mining camps all over the West, there was something to the preacher which went beyond contrived theater. Cord had pretty much decided the man was a touch crazed, and wondered how dangerous he might be.

Paine extended both hands to the shouting miners in supplication and valediction. "Give heed to my words and take them into your heart, lest agony and affliction and torment evermore be your destiny." Righteous mad fire crackled in his dark eyes.

"AGONY! AFFLICTION! TORMENT!" The words exploded from the preacher's mouth like cannon fire.

The crowd erupted into a Babel of hoots and jeers

and shouted hurrahs. Men were pressing toward the buckboard when a gun went off, the sound echoing over them and bringing them to a sharp halt.

Men pushed away from the center of the mass and a few stumbled and went down. A hatless redheaded man in blue cavalry pants with yellow piping stood alone in the clearing that formed. He was holding a Remington Army .44 revolver in both hands.

"Give heed to this, preacher," he hollered.

The man fired again. Paine's flat-brimmed hat shifted a little on his head.

The preacher reached up and took the hat off and stuck his right hand up inside it. His finger protruded from a bullet hole in the center of the high crown.

A low murmur of expectation washed through the crowd.

Paine's deep-set eyes swept over the men before him.

"Will no one disarm this blasphemer?" he demanded. Some of the rich vibrancy had drained from his voice.

No man moved.

"Is this the depth to which you have sunk?" the preacher implored. "Do you take your pleasure in countenancing the intimidation of a man of God?"

The redheaded man grinned with the heady pleasure of his bullying. He took a few steps forward and lowered the .44 so it was aimed point-blank at Paine's heart. "You're full of gas, Bible-Man. You want some ventilating."

Katherine Paine raised her head and took a step back, but she did not seem to be frightened or even particularly concerned. In fact, she wore an expression of bright-eyed expectation, no different from the men on either side of the line of fire.

"Now's the time to start praying, God-Drummer," the man with the pistol sneered. "And you had better hope your Man is listening."

"He is," Paine said, and the black hat fell away from his right hand. Paine swept back the long skirt of his frock coat and the hand came up again faster than a miracle, and in it was a long-barreled revolver, absolutely steady.

Paine fired once and the redheaded man stood a moment before taking a stumbling step backwards. He sat down in the dirt, his legs splayed out straight in front of him like a child in a sandbox. He laid his .44 down beside him almost gently and stared cow-eyed at his right leg. There was a hole in his britches at the knee. Blood bubbled out, floating tiny white shards of kneecap.

Paine swept the crowd with the gun. Someone cleared his throat.

" 'For indeed the hand of the Lord was against them,' " Paine recited, " 'to destroy them from among the host.' " He spun the revolver back into the holster on his right hip. "Deuteronomy, chapter two, verse fifteen."

"Reverend," someone called, "that was fine shooting." The tone held no trace of irony, only genuine admiration.

"You're walking with God, preacher," another man said. He looked down at the man sitting alone in the middle of the street. "Ain't that about right, Haney?"

The knee-shot man looked around blankly. Men laughed.

"Thanks for the sermon, Rev. And the lesson, too."

"Hold!" Paine bent and retrieved his hat, tossed it down to the man nearest the buckboard. "Offerings, to further the Lord's works."

The man with the hat dug down into his britches and fished out currency. He made a show of peeling off a bill and dropping it into the hat. Cord saw no man send it along without anteing up, and when it reached him he dropped in a five-dollar note. Immediately he wondered why he had, and when he looked up Katherine Paine was smiling at him. He felt a bothersome twinge, as though he had been caught with his hand in some cookie jar.

The crowd was beginning to disperse, most of the men heading back toward the saloon. "Jesus and God," the knee-shot man cried out. "Ain't nobody going to help me?"

"Didn't need any help getting where you are." It was the man who had bully-ragged him before. "Which is on your ass. That leg ain't ever going to work right again, Mister Haney. You got years of living as a cripple to ponder on, so's you might as well get started right now." There was more laughter, and the looks men gave Haney as they passed him were full of disdain and empty of pity.

In another minute or so they were gone, all except the Paines and the knee-shot man down in the dirt before them. Cord looked at Katherine, and she gave him a wry smile that seemed to say, *What do you think of us now, Mister Gunman, the dark preacher and his golden lady?* Paine did not notice. He was rifling through the contents of his hat, picking out the dust-laden pokes and hefting them judiciously.

The wounded Haney twisted around to follow Katherine's gaze, stared imploringly at Cord with eyes hollow with agony. The preacher looked up then as well, and when he saw Cord he pointed a long finger of accusation at him. "Evil dwells within thine heart, sir."

Katherine Paine laughed aloud.

All this was going a few steps beyond Cord's taste for the bizarre, and he put his back to their sideshow and headed for the saloon.

Chapter Seven

A T THE GILDED PALACE IT WAS BUSINESS as usual. Cord pushed through the crowd, giving serious thought to a drink of bourbon whiskey and ignoring the sure knowledge that it was a pretty piss-poor

idea, given past history and the present need for a clear
head and time to fit Katherine Paine and her God-
crazed fast-draw husband into the jigsaw scheme of
things. Well and to hell with it, Cord thought angrily.
This time things could sort themselves out.

But before he reached the bar he veered through the
connecting arch which opened into the shabby hotel
lobby. He had not consciously changed his mind, but
something was nibbling at him, some unformed hunch.
Or maybe it was just uneasiness left by what had just
happened in the street, the latest senselessness in a day-
long series.

Whatever, Cord wanted all at once to talk with Chi,
to see if she had come to some insight he had missed.
Could be maybe he just wanted to be with her.

He reached the top of the staircase and turned down
the hall. At the other end, about where Chi's room was,
there was a man in coveralls.

"You there," Cord said.

The man twisted and went for his gun.

Cord was startled, but ten years and more of gunhand experience and a lifetime of instinct acted for him.
His right hand swept back, his stiffened thumb catching
the hammer of the single-action Colt .45 and cocking it
as his fingers wrapped around the grip, his body turning
ninety degrees to thin down the target he presented,
each of the moves natural as life and breathing. The
other man fired but he rushed his shot, and the bullet
gouged into the hallway wall a good two feet above
Cord's head. Cord shot him in the chest without thinking, before the man had time to regret his mistake.

At almost the same instant a shot whined through the
open doorway of Chi's room and thwacked into the
wall opposite. Cord heard the thump of something
heavy and limp hitting the floor.

He moved quickly down the hall and into the doorway without stopping, spinning through and drawing
down with his Colt as he dropped into a sideways
crouch.

Four men were in the room with Chi. Two of them

had their hands full trying to hold her still. It flashed through Cord's mind how strong she was; there had been a time or two when he had to go a ways to get her gentle. The third man was in front of the window, his gun raised butt out, looking for a clear shot at bringing it down on Chi's skull. The fourth man was lying bleeding on the floor.

"Stop it!" Cord ordered. The two men holding Chi looked up at him stupidly, suddenly aware their guns were holstered against a drawn weapon, realizing they were had.

The man at the window tried to turn his clubbed pistol.

Cord shot him in the gut.

The man folded up and crashed back through the window in a shower of splintered mullion and broken glass. Cord heard him bounce onto the canopy that topped the boardwalk, then scrape and bump over the shingles before falling into the street like a sack of potatoes.

Chi kicked back hard and one of the men holding her yelped and doubled up, grabbing involuntarily for his crotch. She yanked her arm free of the other man, rolled across the bed, dropped and was up again on her knees with the dead man's gun.

The man she had kicked in the crotch was still bent over in his pain, and Chi shot him as he danced ineffectually back from her. His partner had his hand on his pistol grip when Chi shot him.

In the close little room the black powder smoke was thick as dawn mist, and for a disorienting moment Cord could only make out vague shapes in the murkiness as he stepped into the room.

"Chi?"

"Here." Some of the smoke began to settle and drift lazily out the broken window, and he saw her dimly as she got to her feet.

"You all right?" Cord asked huskily.

"*Cabrone.* Pigshit son of a bitch *cabrone.*"

"Nolan."

"Goddamned right."

The blood-pumping jag of the fight was easing, and Cord felt icy rage washing in to take its place. Men had just tried to kill his partner.

"Let's get the bastard," he said flatly.

Chi bent over one of the men and pulled her Peacemaker from where it was stuck down the front of his belt. She snapped open the cylinder, rotated it between thumb and forefinger, checking each chamber, then closed it again. Cord was slipping cartridges from the loops in his gunbelt and thumbing them into his revolver.

"Set," he said.

He started to turn for the door, but Chi put her hand on his arm. "They wanted me alive. They figured on having their turns at me before they shot me up for the reward." Her handsome face was a rigid mask. "Now I get my turn with him."

"Sure," Cord said.

The hotel clerk was a rabbity man with tufts of white hair sticking out from the sides of an otherwise bald head. He stood at the foot of the stairs staring up.

"Heard shots . . ."

"No shit," Chi muttered and pushed past him.

They moved under the archway into the saloon, and silence spread out from them to encompass the room. Everyone had heard the gunfire upstairs. It was quiet enough for them to hear the voices drifting in from the street through the batwing doors. "That's Kiner," someone said. "Jesus but they done him good."

The door at the end of the bar where they stood squealed as it opened and Mart Nolan came in, trying to look properly puzzled. "What the hell?" he said. "I heard them shots . . ."

"What were you doing out back?" Cord demanded.

"Holding horses is what he was doing," Chi said to Nolan. He looked at her, his mouth hanging half open. "That's all you ever were, Nolan," she said, "a shit-assed horse-holder, and other men to do your fighting for you. Now you got some fighting to do on your own."

"Lady, you wait a min—"

Chi's gun blurred through the air, and Nolan howled and slapped at the side of his face where Chi's gunsight had ripped into his flesh. Blood stained his grimy fingers.

"You set us up, Nolan," Cord said in a deathly voice. "Just like you did that Culhane kid."

"Except we're not like him, are we?" Chi said.

Nolan stared at her.

"Are we?"

Nolan opened his mouth and could not fashion words.

"You talked reward to some boys," Cord said, "got them to do the rough work. You sent them to the room while you knew I was down the street listening to Paine. You were mostly sure five men could handle one woman, but not so sure you were going to risk getting close yourself. It would not be your neck, no way. You figured to wait it out in back, so you would be in on the gravy if they made it, and clear if they didn't."

"Only it didn't work out, either way," Chi said.

Nolan gaped at the staring faces of the miners in the room, like he expected someone to come forward and side with him. When no one did, he licked his lips and managed to get out a "Huh?"

"They're dead, Nolan," Chi said. "Four of them upstairs in my room, and another lying all broken in the street." Her voice was a harsh whisper. "You are next, *cabrone*."

Cord had never seen her so raging with anger, and understood. It was not the close brush she'd had so much as the fact that they'd gotten the drop on her. That happening, even when she'd got free so quickly, was not something to let pass. And the fact they were trying to take her alive, that was one thing more.

Nolan saw his death in her dark face. He looked past them, raised his eyes to the balcony. "Mister Rawlins," he bleated, "you got no call to set them after me."

Cord half turned, glanced back over his shoulder. Rawlins stood in front of his office, gazing at them impassively. Beside him was Maxwell Prentiss.

And from the corner of his eye Cord saw Nolan—and his panicked awareness it was going to end now and thinking this his last best chance, this moment when Cord was looking away—Cord saw Nolan gasp and go for his gun.

Cord did not move.

Chi shot Nolan full in the face. The muzzle of her Colt was no more than two feet from the bridge of his nose, and at that range the relatively slow-moving and heavy .45 slug seemed to draw all his features into the hole it made, so that the form which fell away from Chi was barely recognizable as anything human.

Cord drew his Colt and covered the room. His rage was gone quick as it came, and he felt for the first time in hours very much in control, released from his confusions by the direct violent action.

"Come on," he said. "Let's get us some answers."

Rawlins was sitting at his desk and Prentiss was bent over him, but he straightened when Cord and Chi came through the office door. There was a pose to their calmness, as if they were expecting this confrontation and had contrived to demonstrate their ease.

"You put out the word on us," Cord snapped.

"No," Rawlins said. "It was Nolan, like you figured. I gave you my oath."

"What's that worth?" Chi spat.

"Five thousand dollars, so far."

"You bought nothing with your five thousand dollars." Cord kicked the door shut behind him. "You keep that in mind."

"What about you, Mister Writer?" Chi said. "Where have you been telling your stories?"

Prentiss put his hands out to his sides, palms out. "Do you think there is still any man in town who doesn't know who you are? What I do doesn't matter."

"What you do," Chi said, "is always going to matter to me. Try remembering that."

"It was Nolan's doing," Rawlins insisted. "But Prentiss is right. Nolan had to nose around plenty before he found five men with the grit . . ."

"Or five men stupid enough," Chi interrupted.

". . . to go up against you." Rawlins shook his head helplessly. "The word is out."

"You knew that?" Cord pressed. "You knew Nolan was opening up about us?"

"Nolan was a fool," Rawlins said, as if that were news. "He was thinking about quick money, but he forgot he was a coward and no man for the job."

"Nolan went gold-simple," Prentiss interjected, "just like all the rest of them out there. But he got it worse than most, and he was a little more simple to start with. Gold has a way of dulling a man's mind."

"You talk too much," Chi said.

"You needn't worry," Rawlins said. "Those miners won't be giving you any more trouble."

"That's a sure bet, Gambler," Chi said.

"We're riding out," Cord told him.

Prentiss smiled slightly and shook his head no.

Cord could see no profit in dragging this out any further. "Adios," he said, and turned his back on them.

"Cash Culhane," Rawlins said. "He's just about due into town."

Cord stopped with his hand on the doorknob. The thing to do was turn that knob and keep walking. It was hard and slick as a riverstone to his fingers.

"What's the rest of it?"

Rawlins held up both hands, as if to show he wasn't palming any cards.

"You'll want to be here," he said. "Take my word on that."

Chapter Eight

CLEAR AS MORNING, CORD RECALLED THE first time.

He was lying flat on his stomach near the edge of the rimrock. From there he commanded a view of near three miles of his backtrail, snaking south through the high-desert mountain country. Cord puffed on a cigarette he had rolled in the saddle before leaving the bay gelding tethered to a juniper back from the edge of the rockfall. He kept the cigarette in his lips, squinting through the smoke at the vast panorama of arid desert shimmering below in the heat.

He saw the rider as he looked up from pinching out the last half inch of butt and stripping the remaining tobacco back into his pouch. The man was maybe two miles back, walking his horse along the faint rocky trace. This was hard country for tracking, and hard on men and their horses too.

The figure was a blur in the shimmering heat waves, but Cord knew well enough who he was. This man had been following them, Cord and Chi, for some days, and it looked as though he planned on sticking. He carried a reputation for finishing out a task when he took it up.

What Cord had realized that morning years before was that this would be a continuing thing, this man and others like him. This one, in his persistence, would sooner or later catch up, and they would face down. One of them would kill the other, with perhaps regrets but no hesitation.

The man was willing, and he was apt.

Maybe as fast and as willing as Cord.

Maybe not. There would be a day to find out. And after that another day and another man, and it would go on like that.

Maybe this was the day to find out about the man called Cash Culhane.

Back in his room, Chi watched him, wary as a cat. "You are getting careless, *viejo*," she said lightly. "Showing your back to a sneak shooter like Nolan."

It would be dark within an hour or so. This far north the days began to noticeably shorten early as August. The hills beyond the western end of town were taking on the burnished sheen of oblique sunset light.

The night would be cool later on, but that was hours away, and now the air was near oppressive as it had been all day. Cord threw open the window of his hotel room and took a deep breath, but the air outside tasted no cleaner or fresher than the close atmosphere of the room. Some of the smoke from the cigarettes they'd been smoking drifted out, and that was anyway some help.

"No," Cord said without turning to her. "You had me covered."

"You'd bet your life on that?"

"Always have. Just did."

From the room next door, Chi's room, came the sound of hammering. The rabbity clerk was nailing planks across the broken window. Cord could not make out the words of the clerk's muttering as he worked, but recognized the tone of fine disgust.

"We could still ride out," Chi said.

"Not me. You know I couldn't."

"No man could stop you."

"That's not the point anymore."

"Yeah," Chi said. "I know."

Cord turned to her finally. "Well sure you do," he said mildly.

Up the street there was no sign of where Haney had lain; horses' hooves had pounded the traces of his blood into the dirt. Cord wondered what had happened to the

knee-shot bully. Did some men finally soften and come
to his aid? Or was he forced to drag himself through the
ruts on his hands and one good knee, hauling his shattered leg behind him like a travois, his teeth clenched
tight and his face specter-white with the anguish of it?
And where did he drag himself?

"I've never run," Cord said, looking thoughtfully to
where Chi lay on his bed. "Not from this sort of face-
off anyhow. I'm not going to start in this shit-hole
town."

Chi reached out a hand and crooked a finger, and
Cord dug out the tobacco pouch and tossed it to her.
She caught it deftly and gave her attention to cigarette
making, letting him have all the time he needed to talk
it out.

But Cord turned back to the window and did not go
on. Chi knew what he was about anyway, and he'd
known for a long time that no man learned anything
new by listening to himself.

There came a point where you could not compro-
mise. By Cord's rules, when trouble came seeking you
in the open in clear daylight—real trouble, as opposed
to mindless pawing and snorting—you faced up and did
not run.

If you broke that rule even once, then none of the
others, or your life, counted for shit. You were no better than some doe-eyed clerk in another man's hardware store, weighing out nails and worrying about ac-
counts by day, and lying with your doughy woman at
night, awake and wondering what it would be like to
have been a man.

When Cord was grown to sixteen and finally shed of
the dirt-scratching east Texas ranch life that was his
bringing-up, as he was working his first cattle drive
from the Nueces River country to the railhead at To-
peka, he had decided on a life of freedom. He could not
abide dwelling in a town, clustered up as if a man had
to be surrounded by other men to face the world from
within the safety of numbers. So Cord went away to the
huge empty country, where a man belonged to himself.

Neither was Cord able to live within other men's laws. By and large those rules were a set of compromises, created out of uncertainty and set down on paper as if that made them truth. They hung like a net over the freedom Cord must have, and seeing that he began to make up his own rules. They were simple and they served: A man did what was right for the time; he did not turn and run; he trusted nothing but his own judgment and hand.

"Pobrecito," Chi said, gently mocking, knowing he was close to a funk and trying to head him away. She handed him the lit cigarette.

Cord thought about their days together, the good and true partner she was and had always been. Other people seemed to see only her dark and angry side. But Cord knew all of her—her loyalty and courage and what she would not stand for—and she stayed with him because he was the only one.

Cord had the sudden impulse to draw her to her feet and hold her, not out of any sexual urge but only to reaffirm what they had. He remembered the touch of her soft skin that afternoon, the warmth of her breath. He stiffened, almost angry. He would not touch her now out of the old fear that such a break might spoil the fine balance of what they had. And maybe he was afraid of something less evident as well.

"Rawlins," Chi said.

Cord relaxed, relieved she had broken the moment.

"That gambler read you right."

"When you work it through," Cord said, "Rawlins doesn't have much to do with what's going to happen." He dropped his cigarette butt and ground it into the floor. Dirt gritted under his bootheel. "But yeah, he read me right."

That afternoon, they could have left Rawlins sitting there with his confident smirk. They could have walked out and gone down through the mass of drinking miners who now averted their eyes from the two gunfighters whose deadly work they had seen close-up. They could have climbed on their horses and ridden out of the hot, dirty, rotting town of Virtue.

But they had not. They stayed and listened, while Rawlins told them how it would be.

"The reason none of the miners will bother you from here on is simple," Rawlins said. "I'm going to give them a reason for keeping you alive."

"You've seen how they are," Prentiss said. He shrugged in deprecation. "They're savages. That's simply a function of gold. But they like their entertainment, and they don't much care what kind it is, so long as it's got something to catch the eye and the baser emotions. You saw how the Reverend Paine and his wife made out. A good-looking woman and some work with a gun is plenty enough."

Rawlins was leaning back in his swivel chair, his delicate gambler's hands clasped behind his neck, and Prentiss was posed by the window, punctuating his explication with his cigar. The two were full of the confidence that comes of holding a lock hand.

"Ladd has been accommodating the boys," Prentiss went on. "He's staged some sporting events—and handled the wagering, of course. He's held prizefights— damned near dead-man fights is what they were—cock fights, and pit bulls going at each other. He brought the dogs up from Denver. Once he sent for a Mexican and staged an afternoon of bullfighting. He killed seven bulls, that Mexican, no trouble at all."

"But the eighth bull won," Rawlins grinned, enjoying himself.

Prentiss puffed out a billow of cigar smoke.

"Tomorrow," he said, "we are having a gunfight."

Chi took an angry step toward the smug writer, but Cord put a hand on her arm. There was nothing to lose in hearing the two men out.

"Max has told you the name of that boy in the saloon," Rawlins said, "The boy's got a brother riding in, and the brother is Cash Culhane. You probably already figured that part out."

"You know the name," Prentiss said. "Most people

in the West do. It's nearly as well known and regarded as the name of Cord." Prentiss gestured with his acrid cigar. "And yours, of course, Miss."

"There is going to be a time," Chi said.

"What sort of time?" Prentiss said blithely. He was the kind of man who would have already blocked out of his mind his humiliation at Chi's hands that afternoon in the café.

"When I bully you around some more," Chi said. "Just for sport."

"I sent for Culhane," Rawlins broke in, "nearly a month ago. There's a part of the story where I left out the full facts. About the road agents, I mean. They tried to take one of my shipments before, and I wired Culhane to come in and stop them."

"Why did you give us five thousand dollars?" Cord asked.

"An investment. I want those hijacking sons of bitches stopped for absolute certain. Long as they are out there I'm hog-tied. You've got an idea of how much gold I'm shipping. Five thousand is cheap enough. Two extra guns, of your class, could only help that much more.

"But there's another reason," Rawlins went on. "Call it a gambler's hunch. I had the idea you might come in handy in other ways."

"What ways?"

Rawlins considered. "In my business some bets are simple as the turn of a wheel or the fall of a card. Others are not so clear. Sometimes you have to wait a spell for the payoff. Culhane's kid brother, the way he was gunning for you, that was pure chance. But I already had my chips down on that layout."

"Make your point."

"I know the shoot-out with the kid wasn't your doing, so does everybody. So will Culhane, but I'm betting he will want to gun you anyway. You after all shot his brother; nothing changes that. I'm going to manage the gunfight, and put up something to make it worthwhile."

Prentiss smiled. "Winner take all—of course."

"Shut up, Max." That crack had been a little strong, even for Rawlins. "My profit comes from a rake on the bets. That's how it works. Real simple."

"You're talking about men facing down for killing and dying," Chi said. "You're meaning to wager on who lives and who gets smoked?"

"It's going to happen," Rawlins said. "It makes no difference whether I bet or not. You know that."

Cord frowned. He didn't like any of this, but Rawlins had the last part right. He also didn't like Rawlins having him figured so finely, so on the money.

"First," Rawlins said, "you know sure as me that Culhane will insist on the fight. You can run but you won't; you're not the running kind. Even if you did, Culhane would follow. And second"—Rawlins held up two fingers—"there's the money."

"Twenty-five thousand dollars to the winner," Prentiss said, "and a fortune in stories for generations to come."

"I figure you have done worse and for less money," Rawlins said.

"No," Cord said. "Not ever anything like this."

Rawlins shrugged. "The more you look at it the cleaner it is. There's no way it doesn't work. You get paid big for doing what you are going to do in any case. And you *will* do it."

Cord saw he was right. The gambler had read him like marked cards in a hand of draw poker.

"He read me all right," Cord said now to Chi, up in the hotel room. "But I'm getting over that. What I cannot stomach is being part of his dog-and-pony show."

"Maybe Culhane . . ."

But Cord was no longer listening. Up toward the western end of town, riders were coming in, emerging out of the setting sun's glare. Chi came to the window and stood beside him, her arm just brushing his.

The riders reached the edge of town and Cord could see them more clearly. Backed by four men, Cash Culhane was riding into Virtue.

Chapter Nine

CORD WAITED ON THE BOARDWALK IN front of the saloon as the five mounted men moved down the center of the street. Culhane, in the lead, scrutinized the shabby town as he rode through it, finally looked at Cord. Cord stood his ground. As much as possible, he had determined to take a hand in how this all went, and he thought it best if the way Culhane found out about his brother was not through a bunch of second-hand stories.

Culhane reined up but did not dismount. The other four fanned out behind him. Culhane nodded and said, "Howdy."

Culhane's men shifted in their saddles, their interest in this meeting vague at best, more taken with thoughts of whiskey and whatever might come with it. Two of them had to be brothers. Both had the same shock of unruly dirty sandy hair and the same coarse features. The older one stared coldly down at Cord, as if to say, *What kind of a man are you?* But his kid brother's face was lit up with a silly idiot's grin that might have meant he was easygoing, or more likely, blood-simple.

The third man was blond, with open handsome square-cut Germanic features. His dress was a mite dandy for the trail: a white Stetson that had been brushed mostly clean of road dust not long before, a sky-blue silk neckerchief, and a rough-out leather vest over a soft buckskin shirt. The last man was a dark squat half-breed, hatless, his long greasy hair tied round with a bandana.

"Go get your drinks," Culhane said, speaking to these men but still watching Cord.

The other three were shifting out of their saddles when the hard-eyed older brother said, "What we got here?" and immediately the others settled back, waiting.

"Looks like one of them bold shootists you hear tell of, Ardee. Wouldn't you say?"

"Looks like, Jake," his brother parroted.

"You two old trail pards, or what?" the older brother said to Culhane. "Or just looking to pass the time of day?"

"You boys see to your own business." Culhane turned in the saddle to give Jake a hard look. "There's plenty of trouble to come, if it's trouble you are itching for." Culhane looked at each man in turn. His tone was quiet, almost gentle. Jake scowled and looked to be toying with the thought of saying something else.

"What is it, Jake?" Culhane said. "Anything that troubles you troubles me. Isn't that right?"

"Nothing." Jake swung down from his saddle without meeting Culhane's look. The other men followed.

Culhane watched from horseback while his men looped their reins over the hitch rack. The one called Jake stared hard at Cord before backing in through the swinging doors to the Gilded Palace. More of the same, Cord thought: another mean and mighty hombre, full of bluster—with guns backing him. Like Mart Nolan. Like lots of other dead men.

Culhane climbed down off his heavy-necked Morgan-cross gray gelding and stood holding the horse's reins. He looked up the street, then called, "You, boy, you come here."

The scrawny kid who waited tables in the café was peering out the door at the newcomers. He shuffled to where they stood, looking sheepish.

"Is there a livery barn in this camp?" Culhane asked the boy.

"No, sir. Got a corral out back of the saloon there."

"Is there anyone watches over it?"

"Yessir. Old Man James. He's too stove-up for prospecting and such."

Culhane dug a gold coin from his britches and flipped it into the air. The boy snatched at it and missed, and it clattered to the boardwalk. The boy picked it up and held it on the flat of his hand, staring as though he had never seen one before—or maybe the coin was easier to look at than Culhane. The gunman's eyes were shocking deep blue, the pupils like drops of incandescent ink.

"You take my horse around to there and you tell Old Man James to pull his saddle and rub him down and grain him, if there is any grain in this place."

"There's grain, mister." The boy held up the coin. "But it'll cost you more than this. This is gold country, mister. Everything is dear." He delivered this speech in the same solemn tone he used in the café.

"That's for you. You tell Old Man James he'll be paid right enough."

The boy took the bridle reins of the Morgan-cross and led the animal around the side of the Gilded Palace. Cord watched all of this with some impatience, wondering if this ritualized attention to his animal was Culhane's way of making some point for his benefit. But then Culhane gestured with a thumb over his shoulder at the four tethered horses and said, "Those boys would be the kind who're more interested in getting their gullets outside some red-eye than seeing to their mounts. This badlands country is poor to chance being set afoot in," and Cord reckoned that was true enough.

"Just between us," Culhane went on, "I wouldn't show my hind end to any one of them. They got the smell of back-shooter to me."

"I thought they were your bunch."

"I haven't got any bunch. There was a job to be done here, and I had to rustle up men quick. Them four is the best I could do."

"I guess," Cord said meaninglessly.

"There anyway aren't so many of the good ones left

nowadays." Culhane shook his head ruefully. "I can't shake the feeling them four could turn bad on a man."

Culhane looked down the street toward the setting sun, now a quarter hidden behind the red-rocked hills. It had no answers to offer. "I expected we'd butt into each other somewhere along the trail, but I wasn't figuring it to be here. I heard tell you were in Owyhee River country, you and the woman, not so long ago."

"We were there."

Culhane pursed his lips, unwilling or maybe too courteous to pursue the subject. "Drink?"

"There's something first."

Culhane stood easy, waiting.

"There was a man in town, more a boy really, claiming to be your brother."

"Yey high"—Culhane held his hand out, palm down—"shy side of twenty, a little quick-draw on the temper."

"Danny is what they called him."

Culhane nodded. Cord wondered if he had an inkling and was going through this act deliberately, making this telling tough as he could; or if this measured easing into things was only his way of playing careful. Cord had determined Culhane was going to get the news from him, but now he wanted it over and done with.

"He called me out," Cord said.

"Dead?" Culhane frowned slightly. "I guess he would be. The damned fool." The frown darkened, but whether that was a reaction to Cord's hand in his brother's death, or to the brother's plain thickheadedness, Cord could not tell.

"This will take some working through," Culhane said finally, and he went past Cord and into the saloon.

For a moment Cord felt something kin to contrition, but it passed. He had done the only thing he was allowed. Culhane would have to deal with it as he saw fit.

After a suppertime lull, the Gilded Palace was now beginning to fill for the evening. The gambling tables were busier than they had been in the afternoon, and Cord counted eleven whores working the floor, trolling

for their first customers. What they did for their gold
dust had the primary thing in common with mining:
Every work shift was hard and long. Four bartenders
jostled one another as they drew beer and splashed whiskey into shot glasses, bottles of amber liquor flashing
in the chandelier's light.

The piano man, in his black bow tie and arm garters
and tinted celluloid visor, looked like any one of a
hundred of his brothers in as many saloons. He was attacking "Sweet Betsy from Pike" on the tinny piano,
pounding out the melody as though he held a personal
grudge against girls from east Missouri.

The door at the far end of the bar was propped open,
and the slight breeze that had come up with sunset was
sweeping some of the unpleasant smell out of the room.
But at the same time it was drawing in a fruity odor of
manure from the corral out back. Still, Cord preferred
the smell of horseshit to the stink of other men's bodies.

Culhane's four men had found a place at the bar.
They stood facing the room, propped back on their elbows with thumbs hooked into gunbelts, surveying the
crowd of miners. They looked to be seeking out the
meanest possible entertainment, or dark mischief; to
men like these, Cord knew, it was all one and the same.
Culhane stood beside them but paid them no mind. He
was hunched over a shot glass of whiskey with the bottle standing within convenient reach, brooding things
out.

At a table in one corner, as far from the bar and the
gambling alcove as they could get, sat the Paines. Maxwell Prentiss was with them, huddled close to the
preacher, their heads bent in confidential conversation.
And to complete the company, Ladd Rawlins was on
the balcony, standing with both hands on the railing
and surveying his business with the satisfaction of a
coyote contemplating a herd of sheep.

Cord found Chi at the end of the bar near the open
back door, toying with a half-full glass of tequila. Since
the events of the afternoon, she was surely one woman
who could drink in this bar without being bothered. A

miner in a gray Confederate army cap shoved down to make room for Cord beside her.

"*Que pasa?*" Chi asked.

Cord shook his head. "His play now."

One of the bartenders came down and set a shot glass and bottle of bourbon in front of Cord and went away again. Cord poured but did not pick up the glass.

"He won't let it lie."

"Most likely he won't," Cord said. "But then we figured on that all along."

"Damn the man," Chi said. "This doesn't have to be."

Cord had no good answer to that. He finally picked up the shot glass and drank, and was setting it down when a voice at his elbow said, "Good evening, folks. Welcome to the party."

Chi did not look around. "What do you want?"

"To buy you a drink," Maxwell Prentiss said. "Why don't you join me and the Reverend and Mrs. Paine, kind of make their acquaintance and friendship? I think you'll enjoy their society."

Chi turned to face him. "We made their acquaintance this morning. I didn't like them any better than I like you."

"Sorry to hear that," Prentiss said, unruffled. "How about you, Mister Cord? Mrs. Paine has been asking about you."

"You go ahead," Chi said, a little quickly and harshly.

"No thanks." Cord was not sure which of this was eating at her.

"There's some things it might profit you to hear," Prentiss pressed.

"For God's sake, Cord," Chi snapped. "Take him away from here."

It was easier than arguing with her, if she wanted to be by herself. Probably she was still feeling nettled over what had happened in her room that afternoon. She could not have liked the memory of those men's hands all over her, knowing what they had in mind. Cord took Prentiss by the arm and led him away from the bar. The writer looked back over his shoulder at Chi. "Does she get that way very often?"

"Only around your kind."

"It must make for some lively times," Prentiss said blandly.

They were at the corner table by then. Katherine Paine looked up and said, "Well, here we all are. Good evening, Mister Cord." She had pinned up her blond hair with three tortoise-shell combs and she wore an unadorned white shirtwaist buttoned to the neck. A long dark linen skirt was draped over her riding boots. Cord thought she looked damned fine.

Cord pulled the empty chair and sat down across from the preacher. Paine took a noisy slurp from a mug of lager, and from the stale-beer odor he was giving off, it was not his first of the night. As if he had divined Cord's thought, Paine looked up at him and said, "The Good Book tells us, 'Drink no longer water, but use a little wine for thy stomach's sake.' One Timothy, chapter five, verse twenty-three."

Prentiss dropped into the seat next to him. "Yeah," he said. "It also tells us, 'The drunkard shall come to poverty, and drowsiness shall clothe a man with rags.'"

"That, sir, is sophistry."

"No it ain't," Prentiss said. "It's Proverbs."

Prentiss winked at Cord, leaned closer, and said, "I used to give temperance lectures, back on the seaboard circuit."

But Paine was watching Cord. Now he placed both palms flat on the table and impaled Cord with a baleful stare. "'The wicked shall perish, and the enemies of the Lord shall be like the fat of lambs. They shall consume; into smoke shall they consume away.'" The preacher's voice was a low malevolent rumble. But then Paine knocked back what was left in his beer mug and waved it in the air for a refill, as if he had lost interest, or perhaps forgotten the rest of them were there.

"Please excuse my husband." Katherine Paine gave Cord a warm smile. "He always turns especially fervent after shooting a man."

"Keep your council, woman," Paine said, but off-handedly, as if he did not really care what she did.

Prentiss put his lips close to Cord's ear again. "The way I figure, our Reverend Paine is about six psalms short of full Psalter."

Cord had already figured that out for himself, but there was still something about the mad minister that bothered him, touching at long-ago and -dismissed uncertainties that now seemed to be clamoring to rise to the surface again.

"Okay," Cord said. "Now that Bible study is over, speak your piece."

Prentiss took one of his cheap cigars from his vest pocket, rolled it casually between his fingers. "Did you talk to Culhane?"

Cord brought his fist down on the table hard, and drink glasses jumped. Katherine Paine stood halfway from her seat and cried out in surprise. Things were trying to slip past Cord again, but he had determined from the time Nolan had pulled his double cross that from then on, he and Chi were running the show as much as they could. In any case this posturing writer Prentiss would call no more shots.

"Okay, okay," Prentiss said. "You've seen him, anyway, and his boys too. Do you know who they are?"

"You tell me."

Prentiss did not look as if he were having so good a time as he'd planned. Some of the smart-assed tone was gone from his voice. "I only know three of them, actually. The brothers are Jake and Ardee Kean. That Jake is the mean one; Ardee is pretty much a half-wit. I interviewed them a couple of months back when they were in the Montana Territorial Prison in Deer Lodge, waiting to be hanged. I got in to see them by bringing the warden two bottles of real Canadian rye whiskey. Jake and Ardee had raped a nester's wife. The sodbuster came in from his fields and took exception, so they shot him and the woman too." Prentiss shot a glance at Katherine Paine. "Sorry, ma'am."

"I don't think so," she said coolly.

"The good-looking one who is so duded up," Prentiss went on, "that's Cooley Gaines. He's a Missouri boy who rode with Bloody Bill Anderson. After the war he signed up with the Union, because it was his only choice other than going to jail as an outlaw. Seeing as how he was such a fine horseman they assigned him to the Seventh Cavalry, but he deserted soon as he got West. He's wanted for that, and for trafficking guns to the Sioux and Cheyenne after Custer ran them out of these Black Hills badlands when gold was discovered here."

Prentiss put his elbows on the table and steepled his fingers. "Fine bunch of boys, wouldn't you say?"

"What about the breed?"

Prentiss shook his head. "I don't even know his name. Maybe he ain't got one. He's just a breed—and you know how they are."

Cord had an idea of what that was supposed to mean—something deeply offensive connected to him and Chi—but he let it pass. This man would keep you insulted all the time, and no other business would ever get done.

"I don't understand Culhane taking up with their no-account kind," Prentiss said, for a moment seemingly serious and even mildly perplexed. "It doesn't figure with his character. Consistency of character, that's the kind of thing a writer keeps in mind."

Cord saw Katherine Paine watching him with a faint ironic smile. He felt something brush his left knee, and then the pressure of a finger, definitely no accident this time, trailing from his knee to the inside of his thigh. Katherine's smile broadened, as if she were challenging him to respond.

Cord left his leg where it was and turned his head toward the bar. Chi was still at the far end, scowling into her tequila, somewhere else from this stinking saloon in this gut-rotted town.

"Listen, Cord," Prentiss broke in. "How do you figure Culhane is taking the news? About his brother, I
mean." His eyes were bright, so Cord knew he had
slipped into his romancer's fantasies again. "I'm pulling
for you tomorrow, don't think I ain't. In fact, that's the
way I'm writing it up."

Prentiss fished in a back pocket of his trousers and
came up with a sheaf of papers, which he unfolded and
smoothed out on the tabletop. A spot of spilled beer
soaked through the middle of one page, but Prentiss
didn't seem to notice. He stared fondly at the first
sheet, scanning a few lines before offering the papers to
Cord.

"This is just the first draft," Prentiss said, "but why
don't you take a look and tell me what you think?"

Cord looked at the man incredulously, but despite
himself he took the wrinkled pages and began to cypher
out Prentiss's ostentatious scrawl:

No sound was heard as the sun rose over the
desolation that is the Badlands country of Dakota
Territory, Sahara of the Americas, where none but
the boldest dare to tread, and from where none but
the most fitly vicious ever return. Even the rooster
feared to crow his raucous welcome to the dawn,
and in their rude shanties men went about their
early-morning ablutions upon their tiptoes.

Both men and fowl knew full-well that the streets
of the cruel gold camp so mockingly named Virtue
would run rivers of blood on this brutal August day.

As the sun reached the apex of its journey across
the cloudless sky, and clocks chimed out the twelve
bells of high noon, two men would face each other,
with steel in their backbones, lightning in their hands,
and black death in their hearts. Two princes among
pistoleros, two lethal virtuosi of Colonel Colt's lead-
spitting instrument, two sultans of the six-gun, would
stride out into the center of the rude berg's street,
and only one would tarry to breathe the salubrious
mountain air another day.

No man of the sturdy miners who comprised the
town's upright and honest populace wished to see

these two potentates of the pistol carry out their mad scheme, but every one of them knew it must needs proceed. For there existed—or so men whispered—"bad blood" between the two sovereigns of the shootists, and nothing but this awful fight to the very death would assuage the savage spirit incarnate in their cruelly beating hearts.

Cord—for that was the name of the younger of the two—was, despite his vicious repute, a courtly and gentle man. Son of a Boston barrister and an Englishwoman of superior breed and noble ancestry, he had left home in his salad days after what should have been a trivial misunderstanding. Young Cord was accused of a theft of which he knew his older, and sinister, brother to be guilty. Though given every opportunity to defend himself, and possessed of an unshakable alibi, young Cord would say nothing to indict the real criminal, for that would be "ratting," and a violation of his code of honor. From such a beginning sprang a life of adventure in the West. Educated in the arts of Messrs. Socrates and Descartes, he became just as thoroughly versed in the arts of Messrs. Smith and Wesson.

Culhane was the coarse cognomen of his antagonist, a crude and repugnant man who was said to have once killed a man when Culhane fired through the ceiling of his hotel suite, as an expedient for interrupting—permanently, as it happened—the other man's anti-morphic snoring. Sired by a brigand who met his fate on the gallows soon after Culhane's birth, out of a woman believed to be at least in part Negro, Culhane was the very archetype of the instinctual and vulgar brute.

The root of this clash of the colossi was said to involve an incident which the reader might consider piddling, but which was anything but to men such as these. Cord was alleged to have taken the liberty of petitioning one Agatha Culhane, chaste sister of the abovementioned, for a dance at a church social. Avering that this was the greatest of insults to every Culhane everywhere, the profane villain struck Cord across the face and demanded the satisfaction of blood in the streets, come morning. The other man, equally steeped in fury . . .

Cord tore the sheets of paper into halves and then into quarters before tossing them across the table at Prentiss. Katherine Paine laughed with delighted surprise, but her husband took no notice, even of the scrap which settled into his beer mug.

"My God, man," Prentiss gasped. He looked like someone who had just had a knee rammed between his legs. "That . . . that was *art!*"

Cord did not know whether to laugh in Prentiss's face or put his fist in the middle of it. He wished he had set the whole damn thing afire. But before he could decide what to do next, the barroom froze to the sound of a high keening woman's cry.

All talk stopped. These were men who had come to depend on a woman's scream as a harbinger of excitement and entertainment. Cord felt Katherine Paine's fingers clamp tight around his thigh, and he recalled her look of breathless anticipation that afternoon, just before her husband shot the man Haney.

The scream had come from one of the whores, a pretty dark-haired girl of about seventeen, only a few inches taller than five feet and very buxom, her breasts swelling above the plunging V neckline of the short-skirted velvet dress she wore. Ardee Kean's thick fingers were digging into her plump bare arm.

Cord felt Katherine Paine's warm breath in his ear. "Cord," she murmured, "do you find her pretty? Would you rather be in her or in me?" Cord spun around, certain he had heard her wrong. Katherine Paine sat back and showed him her faint smile and no other sign, but her hand was kneading the muscle of his thigh.

"No," Ardee Kean shouted at the bar, loud enough for everyone in the room to hear. "You don't say that to me, not ever, you fat bitch. All you bitches think you can do that, but you can't, not none of you. Kill you dead if you say that again."

Ardee's dirty-blond hair was plastered down on his high forehead and his eyes were haunted. There was a thin drool of spittle down one side of his chin.

The woman tried to pull free but Ardee yanked her roughly back, so she bounced up against him for a moment. Before he could shout again, the woman slapped him across the face with her free arm, hard as she could manage.

"Bitch," Ardee screamed, high and hysterical as a woman. "Bitch! Bitch! Bitch!" He shrieked it as if it were the only word he could remember. Beads of saliva sprayed from his mouth.

Men were laughing now, but it took Ardee a moment to hear the sound and realize it was at his expense, he was that lost in his anger. Finally he looked around dully, as if he had forgotten that he and the pretty little whore were not alone. Slowly, as though it took some effort and force of will, the doltish look in his stunned face contorted into rage.

Ardee reached out and grasped the woman's dress at the low V over her breasts and ripped it open to the waist. The woman screamed again, her full breasts bobbing whitely in the chandelier's unnatural light. The miners began to whistle and hoot. "How do you like them puppies, sonny?" someone called from the crowd's anonymity.

Ardee stared down at the woman's breasts, his eyes glazed and his mouth hanging half open, transfixed as a hypnotized chicken.

"What's the matter, boy?" Cooley Gaines pushed himself away from the bar, swaying a little drunkenly. "Ain't you ever seen tits before?"

Ardee gave him a glazed look. He was still holding the girl, and there were splotches of red around his fingers on her soft arm. The look on her face had turned to sullen resignation. She had met the likes of Ardee Kean before.

"Go ahead, boy," Gaines pushed, his voice low and insinuating, bent on prolonging this set-to. "Show us what a hellion you are with the ladies."

"You watch yourself," Jake Kean warned softly.

Gaines ignored him. "You're a red-hot, ain't you?"

he said to Ardee. "You're a hellfiring pistol, is what you are, boy. Leastways with the whores."

"What you talking about?" Ardee sputtered. "You shut that up." He let go of the pretty little whore, and she cradled her big breasts with her crossed arm and scurried away to the far staircase. But she stopped halfway up. Like everyone else she had to see the drama played out.

Ardee did not seem to notice she was gone. He stared at the grinning Cooley Gaines, his eyes and lips wet.

"You ever have a real woman, boy?" Gaines would not let it drop. "You ever have a woman who wasn't some whore? Why'n't you try one, if you're man enough for it?"

He looked past Ardee and heads swiveled to follow his gaze to where Chi was standing alone at the far end of the bar. A low murmur of excitement rose in the room. Most of the miners had seen how Chi had done Mart Nolan that afternoon, and they were doubtless thinking that these new boys did not know what they were sticking their fingers into.

"There's ladies, boy, and then there is whores," Gaines said. "You got to try one that is a lady." He raised his voice in Chi's direction. "Why'n't you try her? You ain't a whore, are you, ma'am?"

Chi did not move or react in any way, except Cord saw her shoulders go tense, and he knew she might be facing Kean and Gaines with her Colt in her hand faster than they could blink. He wondered which way she would go, and he stood in case he needed to back her play.

Ardee was grinning in Chi's direction now. "Yeah," he said. "Why'n't I just do that."

Chi turned then, moving slowly, her hands already hidden under her serape. Cord gripped the butt of his Colt.

But before anyone could make the last deadly move, Cash Culhane stepped in front of Ardee. He put his palm flat on the simpleminded boy-man's chest, not pushing, but gentle as a caress, and he said, "No."

But Ardee Kean was bent on packing a lifetime of poor judgment into one night of drinking. He tried to push the hand aside.

Culhane put his left fist into the middle of the boy's face, a very short hard jab. Ardee yowled like a gut-shot coyote and dropped to his knees on the beer-slick floor, both hands cupped over his face. Blood was spurting from his shattered nose. His shoulders hunched and he began to cry.

Culhane took a step back, and quick as conjuring, his revolver was in his hand and leveled on Jake Kean, whose own gun was halfway out of its holster. Culhane shook his head and said, "No, no, Jake," and Jake let go of his gun, looking for a moment humiliated as a boy caught peeking in some widow woman's bedroom window.

Although Cord had not heard her stand, Katherine Paine was close beside him, gripping his arm in both of her warm hands and whispering in his ear, "When this happens, does your woman get hot afterward? I would get very hot."

Jake Kean was trying to stare down Culhane, or maybe stalling for time, trying to think of some way out of this mess, a scheme where he didn't come out looking backed down, but he failed at both. In his impotence Jake grabbed a fistful of his brother's shirt front and jerked his head up. Ardee's guileless face was streaked with blood and his tears.

"Get up," Jake snarled. "Stop your blubbering."

"Get him out of here," Culhane ordered, suddenly sounding weary. "You too," he said to Gaines and the breed. "You're all of you done for this night."

Miners went back to their drinking and gambling, seeing that this little show would go no further, and disappointed. Nearly simultaneously, but without paying each other any more attention at all, Chi and Culhane turned back to their drinking at their opposite ends of the bar, hunched over their glasses and alone, drawn in to themselves against the rest of the room. Cord knew that Culhane siding with her like that had nothing to do with what was going to happen the next day. Nor did it have anything to do with the death of Culhane's brother. Culhane would have done the same whoever was involved. Those boys were his responsibility, and he was not the sort to stand by doing nothing in the face of such tawdry behavior, surely not from such limber-brained accomplices as the Kean brothers and Cooley Gaines. There was nothing personal to it. Maybe, Cord thought, that was the trouble with all of this.

"Sit down, Mister Cord." Katherine Paine looked up at him. Now nothing in her tone echoed what she had said to him only moments before, but the fire of her sexual excitement blazed in her eyes. A strand of blond hair had worked loose from her combs and hung across one cheek. Cord had the urge to push it back into place. The preacher was staring at the bar through unfocused eyes, as if replaying in his mind the business which had just occurred. Cord wondered how the two of them had gotten hooked together, and to what degree this woman was responsible for her husband's dementia. He imagined the preacher's tapered fingers on the buttons of her shirtwaist, after the shooting in the afternoon.

"He'll pass out pretty quickly now," Katherine whispered into Cord's ear, oblivious of Maxwell Prentiss, who was listening in and leering at them both. "He always does." Her fingers traced patterns on his leg. "Your woman can take care of herself, it would appear."

"She's her own woman."

"How nice. For both of you." Katherine Paine's tongue darted into his ear, quick as a snake's. "You want me, don't you?"

"Yeah," Cord said. He stood up. "But not right now."

Katherine sat back in her chair and looked at him defiantly. "You'll come to me," she said.

Cord nodded noncommittally and wended his way through the tables to the bar, thinking: This business was certainly working through some daydreams.

He could still sense the phantom presence of Katherine's warm hand on his leg, and the moist warmth of her breath as she whispered those things: *Would you like to be in me?*

The bourbon bottle was where he had left it, and Cord poured a glass and put it away, thinking irrelevantly that Maxwell Prentiss had never bought the drink he'd offered. A bartender was hovering nearby and Cord asked him for a glass of water, sipping at it almost daintily when it came. The water had a hard metallic taste to it, and Cord added a healthy shot of the whiskey before sipping at the concoction again. But the brackish well water spoiled the liquor, so Cord took another straight shot into his mouth and swirled it around before swallowing. An old Western lesson, learned again: Never mix the alkaline water into anything but the most awful rotgut.

"La güera," Chi said with no inflection at all. She was still looking down into her glass and her lips barely moved. The blond. Well sure, she had seen him with Katherine. Chi did not miss things, even when you thought her back was turned all the time. Cord wondered if she felt any touch of jealousy, but immediately dismissed the idea. Chi would not, for she knew sure as Cord: that was the kind of thinking, the wrong kind of caring, that could twist itself into imaginary resentments. The two of them covering for each other was the only sure thing in the card game they played. Remember it, Cord told himself, and do not waste conjecture on the rest.

Yet he wondered what Katherine Paine thought of them, what she imagined their life together to be. Did she believe they went from scenes like this back to some hotel room, to mount each other in a frenzy of excitement earned by guns? He wondered if she'd ever shot anyone, and doubted it, for if she had she would know that when the shooting was over the excitement fled—

except for the bystander. Katherine Paine was a kind of perpetual bystander.

She had something in common with Danny Culhane: the spurious need to intrude upon men with whom a person had no business. The Culhane kid had believed power came from the shootist's gun; Katherine Paine believed it came from the shootist's hardness and opening her legs to it, his stiff flesh buried deep inside her.

And what could Chi think of Katherine and her designs, and of Katherine and Cord coming to each other—as all knew they likely would. Cord remembered how Chi had been when they first came upon the Paines that morning, how she had coolly looked the blond woman over in the way Chi had, as if assaying her worth. Long before Cord had ever met her, Chi had determined to live outside other people's standards of petticoated refinement, and since then she had judged other women by those lights.

Cord wondered at reasons, but neither of them was much on prying into the other's past; this was another part of their mostly unspoken agreement. Cord knew Chi had a younger brother who was killed fighting with Juarez's *patriotas* against Maximilian in '67. Like Cord she had spent some time around cows. She could handle the long rawhide riata of the Mexican *vaquero* with as much skill as almost any man. There were occasional times they spent apart, and Cord knew she had kin remaining in Old Mexico. Two winters she had ridden south, gone a month or more each time, while Cord holed up and slowly and carefully drank away the days in some small backlands Arizona town, where the citizens appreciated the money he spent and didn't ask any questions. It was in Mexico Chi had learned to handle a gun and a horse and somebody down there had taught her well, because she was nearly as quick as Cord with the Colt, and really better, more patient, with animals.

Ten years of partnering, Cord thought, and she was still almost as great a mystery as she had been when he had first eyed her, standing against the shadowy wall of the cantina in some nameless Mexican *aldea*. Cord wondered, especially when he caught wind of her sizing up someone like Katherine Paine, if Chi regretted or anyway missed the company of women's society, and came to think that on balance she did not. She and Katherine were not so much different after all, at least in that way: neither of them much wanted women around them.

"Cord." Chi's voice brought him back.

"Yeah?" Cord refilled his shot glass.

"You starting in?" Her tone was mild and without accusation.

"I don't know," Cord said honestly. He picked up the glass but did not drink. The tumbler of water and whiskey mixed was hardly touched. "This damned business," he said suddenly. "Rawlins and his fancy gambler's plans all mixed with Prentiss and his nonsense, and that crazy goddamned preacher. And Culhane and that scum trailing him right into the middle of everything.

"And the woman," Chi said.

Cord drank then. "There's her," he agreed. Cord took out the makings and fumbled at the drawstring of his pouch, aware for the first time that he was a little tight. Chi took it from him, her fingers brushing his.

"None of this is our doing." Chi ran her tongue along the edge of the brown paper, then twisted the smoke sealed.

"No," Cord said. "Not any way you could sensibly track." He struck a lucifer on the seat of his britches and lit the smoke she handed him, then hers. "But that's not the point." A way of seeing it was taking shape in his mind, helped along by the bourbon.

"I've got no wish for a showdown with Culhane," he went on. "I'll go a good deal to avoid it, a long deal farther than I would with another man, because he's all right. But beyond that I'm not going to worry the meaning of it, or what's right or wrong. I'm weary of dwelling on that."

"Easy," Chi said.

"Men get dead that way," Cord insisted, running

through the litany he knew so well. "Spend too much time beforehand fighting your fights over and over in your mind, and you lose when the time comes, because you can't get out of your head. I was never that way and I'm not starting now."

"Okay. It'll be over with tomorrow, one way or another."

"What's that mean?"

"Cord." Her hand lit on his forearm for a moment. "You know where I am in all this."

"Fine."

He was raising his glass when someone tapped him lightly on the shoulder. A big man, Cord's height plus several inches, and broader, was next to him.

"Say, pard," the man said, "I know what dry is. I just come in. I been up on my claim thirty-two days hand-running and nary a pinch of the dust, nor a taste of the panther sweat"—he indicated Cord's bottle—"in all that time. That is what dry is. Dry and busted and looking for high times, that's me."

Cord stared at this new addition to the menagerie.

"I know what dry is, pard," the man said again. "How about sharing that jug o' shine with a bird what's fallen on hard dry times?" The man shifted his weight, set his feet slightly apart, his arms hanging loose and ready.

Cord set down his glass, gave the big man a neighborly smile, and said, "No."

The big man gave the smile back. "Well now," he said, "I'm too dry to be asking. I'm an egg that takes what he wants."

He reached for the bottle.

Cord put his left fist into the man's stomach and brought his right up to meet the man's jaw as it came down. The man straightened and threw out both arms and crashed back over a tabletop, wood splintering and glasses and cards scattering under his weight and momentum. The four men who had been sitting at the table looked down at the big man lying unconscious at their feet.

Cord turned back to the bar, refilled his glass and drank.

"You feeling better now?" Chi asked, amused.

"Yeah," Cord said. "I guess I am."

Chapter Ten

CORD LAY ATOP THE BED IN HIS UNION suit. He held the bourbon bottle loosely by the neck. It was still about half full, and every once in a while he would take a shallow sip. A night breeze drifted in through the open window, and Cord reckoned that pretty soon it would be cool enough for sleep.

He had drawn up the chair for a night table. His makings lay upon it next to his holstered Colt. He gave some consideration to rolling a smoke, but decided it would be more work than it was worth. Down on the street a man let out a braying laugh, but the town was gradually quieting down.

Cord could hear Chi moving around next door. The wall between the rooms was only a single layer of badly joined planks. She whistled a quick trill of notes as she kicked out of her boots, and Cord imagined her funk had passed, along with his own uncertainties. After a time the whistling stopped and the light cracking through the gaps in the wall went out. Cord dozed and saw himself.

They had been riding some time, but Chi had been drawing farther and farther ahead, so she crossed the little rocky creekbed while Cord was so far back he could barely make out her figure. He was suddenly afraid she was going on without him, and he spurred his bay gelding, but the horse only snorted and plodded on at the same stolid pace. Cord looked up again and was relieved to see Chi still in view. She had dismounted on the far grassy side of the creek and was standing beside a wide pool where the water was slow moving and blue as the pale sky.

It took forever to reach the creek, and then the gelding would not cross. The animal touched a forefoot into the water and drew it out again, and all the while Cord felt himself increasingly powerless—until finally he was outside himself and watching as he cursed and raked at the gelding with his spurs. Still the horse would not move on. Cord dismounted and tugged on the reins. Chi was calling something, and although he could not understand the words, Cord knew she wanted him to leave the animal and come along on his own. For some deep reason, that was out of the question, and Cord pulled with all his strength on the bridle, but the gelding seemed to have taken root. When Cord looked again the horse was indeed made of hard, dark close-grained wood, and Cord was a small boy, and Chi was looking across the water to him with vast regrets.

Then she remounted and backed her mare away, so Cord could still see her face. But he could not bring himself to cross the creek and join her. She turned the mare finally, and he watched until she disappeared into the sun's glare, and tasted hot saltiness on his lips . . .

Cord opened his eyes and silently located the holster in the darkness. There was someone in the hallway outside his door. He drew the Colt and held it loosely, his arm lying out straight on the bed next to his body.

Whoever it was knocked, so softly it was barely audible. Cord waited. The knock came again, and after a pause, the scratching of a key in the doorlock. Cord thumbed back the hammer of the revolver.

The door opened about halfway and a figure slipped through in the lash of light from the hallway. The door closed again and darkness swallowed the room. In the dim indirect light from the street Cord could make out the figure against the far wall.

Cord struck a lucifer on the bottom of the chair and lit the coal-oil lamp setting on it. When he turned down the wick, smoky fingers of light drew in toward it.

Katherine Paine stepped forward into that light. Cord showed her the Colt before pointing the barrel at the ceiling and gently letting the hammer back down. Katherine watched, smiling whitely.

"I didn't know," she said. "I thought you might be with her. She acted like she wanted you."

You don't know a thing, Cord thought, but he let it go. There was no point in explaining what was none of her business in the first place.

"That funny bald man downstairs gave me the key. It cost me twenty dollars."

Cord grinned. "You figure you're going to get your money's worth?"

"After a time."

She came over beside the bed and stood a moment looking down at him. She was still dressed in the shirtwaist and linen skirt she'd worn in the saloon, and she had added a knit shawl over her shoulders against the coming of the night chill. She sat on the edge of the bed next to him, then leaned in and kissed him, her breasts soft against his chest. Cord started to put his arms around her, but she pulled away and sat back up again.

Cord groped on the floor and found the whiskey bottle, pulled the cork and took a shallow sip, then passed it to Katherine. She hesitated, then took it and tilted it full back. Her boldness in the early evening had seemed strange and exaggerated in some game-playing way, and now she was acting backed-off some, and drinking as if to stiffen up her courage. But she had gone to the trouble and expense of getting into his room, and the whiskey in Cord had calmed and warmed him. Tomorrow was a long time off. He was willing to pass some little while waiting to see what exactly this woman was about.

"Can you roll a cigarette?" he asked.

"I used to for my father." She picked his pouch off the chair seat and turned it in her hands without opening it. "But that was quite a few years ago. He died when I was a girl."

She stared into the memory for a moment more before drawing the pouch open and fishing out the brown papers. Cord figured all this was leading to something besides lovemaking, but there was whiskey to pass the time until it got to that.

"I married him eight years ago in Saint Joseph, Missouri," she said all at once. "He was the pastor of the Second Methodist Church, and nothing like the way he is now."

The cigarette she was working on tore, and she shredded the tobacco back into the pouch and began over again. "He lived a life of preaching goodness and reverence, birthing and burying and matrimony, and the comforting of widows. My mother was among them, and after he came calling the first time he started coming back every week. He'd talk to my mother about God's will and His greater plan for man and the eternal paradise He reserves for the righteous, among whom, he assured her, my dead father was surely numbered. I turned seventeen that summer."

Katherine Paine's second attempt produced a tolerable smoke, better anyway than Cord could have made. He leaned over the chimney of the lamp and drew fire into it.

"We heard about the gold strikes all the time. Pilgrims would come off the riverboats at Saint Joseph to travel out overland, and we were all used to the wild stories of nuggets big as pumpkins and creeks whose beds were pure gold dust. Zachariah would bless the pilgrims and wish them Godspeed, and go quietly back to his regular flock.

"And then," Katherine said, "three years after we were married, a man named Micah Kane came to the house. He had grown up in town, but a year before, he'd left for California and gold. Kane had worked, on and off, as a furniture maker, and he left a wife and three little daughters behind. They ended up living on the poor fund. Zachariah thought Micah Kane had come to ask his help in confessing his sins and begging the Lord's forgiveness, but that wasn't any part of it."

She took another long pull from the whiskey bottle. Cord took it from her and drank too. "Kane pulled a sandalwood cigar box from his satchel and set it on the table and said, 'Open it up. Go ahead and take a look.' When I did, it was filled with gold, dust and flakes and one nugget nearly big as a plum."

"And your husband took one look and got the fever."

"Yes," Katherine said without surprise at Cord's perception. It was a common enough story, though it did not usually include a preacher. "His face went pale as if he'd seen the Holy Spirit—which in a way I guess he had—and then it turned flushed, and the fervor in his eyes was pure gaslight madness. I was frightened. I thought he had been literally possessed. A sudden presence of evil had come into the room, I felt it, like a slow shutting out of the air.

"Micah Kane had come to gloat. He thought he had the right. A week before his family had been the shame of the town. Now he was going to be a leading citizen. When he left, my husband slumped into his chair and stared blindly at nothing. He didn't move until I came to call him to his supper. Then he looked up and said, 'The wages of sin,' and I knew what he was thinking: If a godless blasphemer like Kane could strike it rich, what were the rewards of a pious man?"

"It never has worked out that way, far as I could see," Cord said. "Goodness and gain hardly ever have much to do with each other, and thinking they do won't make it so."

"He never learned that." Katherine watched Cord stub out his cigarette. "I don't think he was ever completely sane afterwards." She smiled then at some unvoiced memory. "We left Saint Joseph the next week, after dark, so Zachariah would not have to explain to his flock that their minister had lost hold on what was real. My mother was dead by then, so I had to go with him, and really I wanted to. Going West seemed such a grand adventure. Can you understand that?"

"Yup," Cord said.

"We went to the Sierra Nevadas in California for a time, and later we tried the Tahoe high country, and near the Divide in Colorado, and the desert outside Tombstone in Arizona. Before coming here we were in Last Chance Gulch in Montana Territory. Always there was gold and miners and sinners all around us, and one stuck to the other like flies to window glass, but we never struck anything that panned more than two ounces a day and that was only once. It ran out in three weeks. The longer our bad luck held, the greater my husband's madness grew."

She was staring into the shadow of the far corner of the room now, deep into her story. "We had to eat. Zachariah began to preach sermons like the one you heard this afternoon, full of hellfire and damnation. When he was finished he passed the hat, and it always came back full. Zachariah had found his true calling. These miners are willing to pay for entertainment, and besides, you live by your luck and you don't want to take any chance of insulting the Lord.

"The first time I heard him do it, though, I was frightened out of my wits. Before the sickness got him, his sermons had been full of gentleness and reassurance. Now they are dire threats and apocalyptic predictions, and they should sound like the nonsense they are, made up to give the miners their money's worth. But they are more than that. He has the power to convince men, and he holds that power over them. He is able to show them he really does know something they do not, something eldritch and terror-filled. You felt it. I was watching you, and I could see it in your face."

"Yeah," Cord said. He took a pull on the whiskey. "But for right now I've decided not to worry about it."

"It was his idea to stand me up there like you saw me. He knew it would draw them in. But by the time he

hit on it, there was more to it than crowds. He had begun to believe his own sermons, including the part . . .
what he said about women.

"And I liked it," she said, "I liked standing there
with those men looking at me. That was the strange
part: I discovered I loved having those men see me. I
hate what he says, but I like to think about some man
like you."

She laid a hand on Cord's chest and pushed his union
suit off his shoulders. "And there's another reason," she
said. "He hasn't touched me in two years." Her voice
had gone soft again, reminded of why she was here.
"He saw the sight of me as an abomination. When I
was naked, I mean," she murmured. Her lips were close
to Cord's. "I want you to see me. You tell me what you
think."

"Take off your clothes," Cord said.

She stood up and pulled off the shawl and draped it
over the back of the chair. Cord drank and watched her
slim white fingers work at the shirtwaist's whalebone
buttons. "I could have left him many times," she said,
shrugging out of her blouse. "But there was no place
for me to go. And in the gold camps, places like this, I
did not see men"—she smiled—"men like you, who
suited my taste."

She reached down to the hem of the long skirt and
pulled it over her head. Beneath she wore a white cor-
set laced up the front, pushing her breasts up and out,
nipping in at the waist before flaring at her hips. Her
legs were long and elegant.

"There's more," she said, suddenly somber. "I . . .
he frightens me. He's becoming more and more strange.
I'm afraid he'll do something . . ."

But Katherine Paine did not strike Cord as a frightened woman.

She fumbled at the laces while Cord lay back and
enjoyed watching this body of hers revealed, and she
watched him look at her. Her breasts were high and full
and Cord stared longer at her stomach, rising and falling as her breathing came more quickly. Cord pulled

off the union suit and blew out the lamp as she came into bed beside him and laid the length of her cool body against his, her hands working at his chest and stomach.

"After it's over," she whispered in his ear as she reached lower to touch at him, "I want to go with you." Cord frowned into the darkness, though he had been expecting something like this. "You don't have to stay with me. Just take me to a city where I can start again . . . without him. Take me to Denver, or even Cheyenne."

Then she lay quiet, running her fingers back up over his stomach and shoulders, toying with his nipples as she waited for him to speak. When he did not she said, "I can pay you. He has money, plenty of it. We can take it from him, you and I."

"How's that?" Cord said, startled at the last part.

"Isn't that what you do anyway?"

Rather than reply Cord pulled her on top of him, and immediately her hand slid between them, and Cord felt himself glide up into her, her smooth white bottom moving slowly in the dim light of the street which cast into this room. Then she was moving more quickly, and after a time she began to gasp as if the night air had gone thin. Cord went tense for what seemed a near endless moment, and then the release flooded through him and into her, and her gasp dissolved into a series of quick satisfied yips.

When she stopped she let her full weight down on him in drained exhaustion, and she fell asleep almost before he'd gone limp, curled against him and breathing heavily on his shoulder. Cord regarded her in the dim light and wondered if in some unaccountable way, years of living with madness had taught her a shortcut path to the tranquility of dreamless sleep.

Chapter Eleven

CORD STARED DOWN AT HIS EIGHT DOL-
lars' worth of fried eggs. The eggs stared back. He
stabbed a fork into one yolk, then carved off a piece of
ham, stacked crispy egg white on it, and used the combination to mop the runny yellow. The ham was tough
and dry, but the warmth of the food gradually worked
to awaken him to the day. *"Bueno,"* he grunted, and
Chi nodded and shot him a grin. She was going easy
on him this morning.

But Cord was feeling mainly fine anyway. He had
awakened in the middle of the night for no reason beyond awareness of the full-bodied woman in the bed
beside him. He aroused her with his hands, and this
time it seemed to go on for a long time, maybe blending
back into dream-rich sleep before he surfaced for the
ending.

Cord awoke for good at dawn, a habit from old
ranch-kid days and springs on the cattle trails, which he
had never been able to shake. He had grown up on
short rations of sleep, and always more work than daylight hours. So now, even in his leisure, five or six
hours seemed all that patience could endure.

Katherine was gone. Cord felt clearheaded and emptied, everything swept from his mind but the business of
the day. It was a comfort to be able to perceive events
in a simple straight line again. The fried eggs had a rich
meaty flavor. They tasted of strength.

Katherine came into the café when Cord was halfway finished with his meal, trailed by the preacher. She smiled at Cord, then turned the smile on Chi for a moment, who surprised Cord by returning it.

The Reverend Paine looked god-awful, like a man with the great-grandfather of all hangovers. He was unshaven and his face glistened with sweat. His black frock coat and trousers were dusty and rumpled, as if he had slept in them, on the ground. There was a vacant beguiled look in his sunken eyes, like he was hypnotized or clear gone into some private vision of his own invention. He followed his wife to a table in the corner, and when he sat and put his arm on the tabletop his hand began to twitch like a toad. The dozen or so miners at the three other tables were turning their heads from one to the other, uncertain which was the more interesting: the tetched beer-soaked preacher, his pale wife, the calm dark gunfighter, or his woman. Paine did not notice them, or even seem to have much clue to his whereabouts.

Chi said nothing until they had finished the last of their ham and eggs and the scrawny boy had cleared the plates and brought more coffee. Then, after she'd rolled and lighted the smokes, she said casually, "They say there's cattle coming in to Miles City over in the Montana Territory, now that the railroad has come through that far. That's only maybe four days' ride from here."

"Some number of herds?" Cord asked judiciously, as if this were going to be a matter for careful but immediate deliberation and decision.

"That's what I hear."

"Cattle means money."

"And money means banks. *Que dice?*"

"Sure, we'll head that way," Cord said. "That would be real relaxing, a look into a bank, after all the fun in this Virtue town." He grinned at Chi and she grinned back, and made to answer.

But then she saw Cord's smile drain off as he looked past her toward the cafe doorway. Cash Culhane was standing just inside.

"But then," Cord said, "I guess you recollect Carson City well as I can."

Culhane moved across the room toward them, nodding his good morning. Chi looked up at him and frowned.

"Yeah," she said. "I recollect Carson City."

It had been two years back and springtime when they rode in to the Nevada country below the Sierras, where the snow was still lightly traced on the fir trees in the mornings. That year had been a good one for the range around there, plenty of run-off from high snow in the mountains and a mild winter down in the meadows. Following the spring drives over to the cities of California, after the passes were open, the members of the Nevada Stock Growers' Association had holed up in the Carson City Social Club to drink whiskey, swap lies about the early days, and pow-wow regarding problems with nesters who were moving in by the handsful, especially around the Humboldt River valley and thereabouts, homesteading what had by long tradition, since the days of the wagon trains, been open free range. So far the nesters were not a problem of serious proportion, and the middle-aged men who had grown wealthy off that land aimed to see they did not become one.

Cord and Chi had no interest in the troubles between the settlers and the stockmen. They had been drawn to Carson City by the safe behind the front desk on the first floor of the club, in which the proceeds for several large livestock sales were resting for the duration of the Nevada Stock Growers' get-together.

According to Mercury Mike Callahan, the total amount in the safe might come to one hundred and twenty-five thousand dollars, in nice round figures.

Mercury Mike had specialized in safes and strongboxes before a trigger-quick deputy town marshal in Yakima, Washington, put a .44 slug through his right hand. The hand healed up enough so Mercury Mike got back his touch, but by the time he was out of the territorial prison in Walla Walla he was too agey for the

rugged life that was part of the outlaw trail. Now he
was sixty-three years old and working as the swamper
at the Carson City Social Club, and he did not want to
die cleaning up other people's messes. So he had cy-
phered out the combination to the safe and passed it to
Cord and Chi, for a one-third share of the take.

They rode in the day before they planned on pulling
off the job, and they had not been in town two hours
when they ran into Cash Culhane.

Cord had known the name of course. Culhane was a
Texican like Cord, and according to the story he had
been a Ranger for ten years. Some said he was cash-
iered out when he shot a man who had killed a ranch
family of seven before rustling their livestock, instead of
bringing the man in to face courtroom justice. But others said he had just up and quit when he discovered he
wasn't cut out to do things on other men's schedules in
other men's ways.

Since then he had taken various jobs which called for
a man with stiff nerves and fast hands. There was talk
he had done his share of thieving, too, but no one could
name for certain a place where he was wanted nor a job
he had for sure pulled off. Then, too, Culhane was a
close-mouthed man and not given to blowing his own
horn, and for sure not the sort a smart man would want
to talk against, not where he was apt to be heard.

Now Culhane was in Carson City working for the
Nevada Stock Growers' Association. They called him a
range detective and made a lot of public noise about the
depredations of rustlers on the open grazing land. But it
was common knowledge—or at least most men were
pretty certain—that Culhane's real job was driving out
the nesters, by whatever means it took.

Chi and Cord went into the Carson City Social Club
the next night, two hours after sundown. Mercury Mike
did not come in until eleven. It was agreed he would
have nothing to do with the actual job. Besides, he told
them, nine was the best time, late enough so the supper
crowd was done with, and early enough so the serious
carousing would not yet have started.

It began smoothly enough. Chi and Cord came in the back door on the alley which ran off Clay Street, and in through the deserted pantryway off the kitchen, following the floor plan of the club which Mercury Mike had sketched. The pantryway opened into the dining room, and through an archway and down a short hallway was the reception desk, fronting on the manager's office.

The clerk was a thin sallow-faced man of about forty. He looked up and saw two guns pointing his direction. All he said was, "Damn," in a tone of mixed frustration, impotence, and awe. Chi gestured with her Colt toward a chair in the office back by the safe and out of sight, and when the sallow-faced man sat down they did not take the time to tie him but only stuffed a bandana in his mouth. Upstairs, according to Mercury Mike, there was a billiards den and a smoking room, and men would be spending time there, getting started on the drinking which would occupy the night. Noise down here was something Cord and Chi did not need.

The safe stood waist high and was enameled black, except for a hand-painted auburn nameplate which read, "Rossbach Laminated Strongbox Company, Lowell, Massachusetts, U.S.A." Cord spun the dial three revolutions to the right to clear it, then clicked it back and forth to the numbers Mercury Mike had given him. When he turned the handle the latch bar slid free smooth as glove leather.

Cord had just stuffed the first handful of cash into his satchel when Chi whispered, "Trouble." Cord straightened and pressed himself to the wall beside the office door, and waited.

From the vicinity of the front desk a man's voice said, "Jefferson!" And then more softly, "Where the devil is that man? You can never . . ." The sentence trailed off.

Chi nodded toward the safe, but Cord had already figured out that part. A man standing at the desk could see its thick iron door standing open. In about one heartbeat the man would holler for help.

Cord drew his Colt and spun into the open doorway,

holding down on the man across the waist-high desk, five feet away. The man was about fifty, sleek and well-fed by the look of him, in a spotless new Stetson and a broadcloth coat over a vest and a linen shirt.

"Hold it," Cord ordered. "Right there."

"Shit, son," the man said conversationally, "I spent the first thirty years of my life facing down white men, Indians, and critters, and any one of them a hell of a lot tougher than you look to be. Hard to scare a man after he's come through those days."

"You listen, old man . . ."

"Nope," the rancher said. "You listen." His right hand came up from behind the counter and Cord caught a glimpse of a little Remington Elliott .22 five-shot deringer before the man fired.

The bullet thudded harmlessly into the door jamb next to Cord. A one-inch barrel didn't much make for accuracy, but the shot was plenty loud enough. Running footsteps thumped on the ceiling over their heads. The stout man opened his mouth to cry for help, and Cord lunged across the countertop and laid the barrel of his Colt against the cattleman's head. The man went down in a heap. But somewhere near the end of the hall, men were coming down a staircase.

"That tears it," Cord said, grabbing for the satchel. *"Vamonos!"*

Men rounded the corner at the far end of the passageway, and Cord put two shots in their direction, high enough not to hurt anyone, before darting after Chi along the pantryway and out to where they'd tethered the horses. Nobody followed for a moment. Rich men, Cord reflected, were a lot less willing to risk their lives for money. He and Chi were traveling at a hard spur-jabbing gallop and a hundred yards down the alley before anyone ventured out of the Carson City Social Club, or fired a shot. They were away clean, or so it seemed.

Just on the chance of something going real wrong, they had stashed provisions off to the north in the high desert country west of Pyramid Lake. No one tried to stop them as they galloped through the streets of Carson City, but they spent the rest of the night in the saddle anyway and had got themselves north of Reno by sunrise. Such bearing on and caution had proved its worth many times. This turned out to be another of them.

They stopped a few minutes after first light. Cord built a fire big enough to boil coffee, pouring water from his canteen into the little white-enameled pot and throwing in a half fistful of grounds. It was just beginning to bubble, the aroma cutting into the chill morning air, when Chi called to him.

She was standing near the horses on a rise that commanded a panoramic view of the long dry lake bed they had just ridden up out of. Off at least five miles along the trail they'd cut was a rise of dust not quite obscuring the flash of movement. Cord dug his spyglass out of his saddlebags, extended it, and screwed his eye up to the object lens.

"That damned Culhane," Chi guessed.

"That's right," Cord said. "And six men riding along with him."

He lowered the spyglass, thoughtfully polished at the lens with a corner of his neckerchief.

"Well sure," Chi said. "Why not? He would have got up a bunch. And of course he's the one they'd set on us." She didn't look a damned bit happy.

Cord got out the satchel and looked at the money they had been able to get hold of before the trouble intruded. There was something like three thousand dollars, total. That came out to a thousand apiece—Cord and Chi, and a one-third cut to be sent back to Mercury Mike Callahan. It looked like the old peterman's bar-swamping days were not yet over.

As for him and Chi on this run across the dry Nevada highlands, Cord had no doubt they would work damned hard—a thousand dollars' worth, for sure—for their shares.

He was right enough about that. They rode all that day and the next, stopping only when the horses abso-

lutely had to have rest, dozing in the saddle when they
could. But there were at least two things working on
their side. To begin with, there was the food and water,
and feed for the animals, which they had stocked out
ahead. Second, their horses, Cord's long-reached bay
gelding and Chi's big mare, were blooded and fed up
strong, and picked for their traveling endurance. It was
a safe guess that none of the men in the posse were as
well mounted.

Except maybe for Culhane. He was the professional—like them.

There was the main card against them: Cash Culhane. If the stories that came with the man had any
truth to them, he would not quit, and he would be astride
a going horse. The others might drop out—probably
would after a time—but not Culhane.

It turned out that way. On the morning of the third
day Cord looked back over another of the long valleys,
sagebrush and alkali reaching to blue mountains on the
day-away horizon, the shadows of cloud moving over it
like loneliness, and Cord saw Culhane was still coming.

Now he was alone.

"The rest of them must have turned," he told Chi. "I
figure they got to a place where going afoot in the desert was looking like a possibility, and more than they
signed on for." It was country where a man walking
could die, and would at least suffer in ways for which
no reward could compensate.

Cord watched as the lone rider came on, walking his
horse across the glaring white edges of an alkaline
playa, the lake dry except toward the center where a
muddy smear of spring water glimmered in the sun.

"But not Culhane."

"No," Cord said. "Not Culhane."

Cord's bay gelding was showing signs of heavy weari-
ness, his head drooping as he walked, eyes going dull.
This kind of traveling could not go on much longer.
The heat rose in shimmering sheets off toward Culhane
and his figure wavered in the light like it might vanish.
But Cord knew it would not. He swung back into the

saddle and pointed the gelding off toward the rocky ridge toward which they were climbing.

"We're going to have to do something."

"Yeah," Cord said.

Cord found what he was searching for soon after noon, on the other side of the ridge. Here the trail cut down steeply for a few hundred yards through a narrow defile, a dry wash carved through the lava rock by a creek or glacier eons in the past. The walls rose maybe sixty feet on either side, and the passageway between was no more than wide enough to ride through.

A fine place for an ambush, and for that reason Cord thought it unlikely Culhane would ride into it. The manhunter would spend time thinking it out and searching for a way around, and while he did he would be atop the ridge, with little cover.

Cord found a place for himself on the rimrock above the defile and carefully hid his horse. There was time enough to smoke a cigarette before Culhane appeared on the ridge, maybe a hundred and fifty yards away, silhouetted against the white desert sky.

Cord waited, cursing himself for the carelessness of smoking. Hopefully Culhane smoked as well, and so would not notice the faint drifting odor of burning tobacco. After a few moments, Culhane moved his horse tentatively forward, cutting the distance between them by maybe twenty-five yards before he reined up again. This time he sat the animal quietly and squinted into the sun.

And he did smoke. While Culhane's hands were busy building a cigarette, Cord stood and brought his Winchester to his shoulder. He knew Culhane would catch the motion from some corner of his awareness.

"Sit easy, Culhane," Cord called. "Keep those hands where I can see them."

For a moment Cord thought the other man had not heard. Culhane finished rolling the cigarette, licked at the paper, stuck it into his mouth. Moving with elaborate slowness he fished a lucifer from his shirt pocket and struck it on his saddle horn. He cupped his hands around the fire and held the tip of the smoke in its flame. Only then did he look up toward Cord.

"That's a fair piece of rifle shooting you're thinking to try," he shouted. He took the cigarette from his mouth in another cautious movement. "You think you can make the shot?"

"Don't even want to find out," Cord called back.

Culhane nodded, as if that were a satisfactory answer.

"Ride up to the head of that canyon," Cord directed. "Be sure to keep those hands up and clear."

Chi came out from behind a pile of lichen-etched lava boulders to back Cord's play. When Culhane saw her he said, "Howdy, Miss," and something softer to his horse. The animal stopped and put his nose down to the dirt. Chi stood maybe twenty feet away, her Colt steady on Culhane.

The ride had taken its toll on the older man. Culhane's face was blotched and peeling with patches of raw skin, and his lips were puffy and cracked. His mount looked equally hard used, worn down and trembling, near to exhaustion.

Without taking her gun off Culhane, Chi stepped back to her mare and unlooped her canteen from the saddle horn. She tossed it to Culhane. He caught it, his horse shying a little sideways, took several shallow sips, then capped it and offered it back. Chi shook her head. "Obliged," Culhane said.

"Do you want my guns?" He looked up at Cord.

"I want your word," Cord said. "You can keep the guns."

"How's that?"

"You're riding back. That's the way it is."

"You figure?" Culhane said.

"We got no wish to see you dead," Cord said. "Not from killing you, nor from you running your horse to death in this desert. A man could die in this stretch if he doesn't know the water. You ride back, and you let us be."

Culhane seemed to consider the proposition.

"Maybe," he said finally. But then he shook his head. "You got to hand that money back."

"That's not going to happen," Cord said. "You know that."

"Too much talk," Chi snapped. "Let's get on with this."

"You got no choice, Culhane," Cord said from the rimrock. "You will give us your word, and you are going back to Carson City with empty saddlebags."

"Or your trail ends right here," Chi added, waving the barrel of her Colt.

Culhane frowned at her, turned the gaze on Cord. "I reckon that is the way of it," he conceded. He set his shoulders. "You have my word: I'll not follow you any further—anyway not on this trail."

"Not on any trail," Cord said. "Jesus Christ, man, it's only three thousand dollars."

Culhane grinned a little, looking up to Cord and squinting against the pale glary brilliance of the cloudless sky. "But that don't mean this is done and finished. This sort of set-to, men trying to stare each other down over gunsights, it has a way of getting settled for good and sure, somewhere down the line." Culhane turned his horse back toward the south, but kept his eye on Cord. "So long." He nodded at Chi, almost courtly. "*Hasta despues.*"

All that was long miles and years in the past, and Cord would not dwell on what might have happened. But out on that northwestern Nevada desert under the enormous white-edged bowl of perfect sky, he'd had the feeling Culhane was right. And now, here in this dirty Dakota gold camp, he was certain of it.

Chi looked up to the older man, Culhane, as he stood there by their table in the little café, and said, "Set with us."

Culhane touched two fingers to his hat brim. "Yes, ma'am."

Morning dawdled as Culhane ordered beefsteak and eggs, no potatoes. "They got the worst goddamned hashed spuds I ever ate," he said when the food came, talking to no one in particular, concentrating on his plate. No one said anything else. Culhane drank a pot of black coffee with his breakfast, then shared another pot with Cord and Chi while they all digested.

Instead of being awkward, the silence was somehow comforting to Cord. Culhane was nearly finished eating before he realized why. The three of them, him and Chi and this other man, were bonded together whether they wished to be or not, and this meal together was a rare occasion. In this town, populated by miners and gamblers and frauds, and hooligans and parasites of every stripe, Culhane was the only man with whom Cord could feel any kinship. They were in agreement on one unspoken thing: the need to be independent and without fear. They were men who had determined on such behavior early on, and that decision irrevocably colored everything else.

So for this brief time they had a basis for friendship, and the ease of a peaceable meal. But in a few hours they would be contesting over that same creed of personal freedom, neither man able to back down . . . Cord refilled all three coffee cups. Culhane would be thinking the same way—wouldn't he?

The other man slid his plate away and cleared his throat. "Last night . . ." he began, and it was the first time Cord had seen him ill at ease.

It tickled Chi. Cord could see that she liked this man in her way. "What about last night?" she asked, almost gaily.

"Them boys," Culhane said ruefully. "Gaines and Kean and his cow-minded brother. Gutter trash."

"They're your bunch," Cord said flatly.

"Yeah," Culhane said into his coffee cup. "That part is setting less and less easy with me. I'm worried they are going to turn bad on me, and then . . ."

"How do you figure?" Chi asked.

"It's nothing I can put a rope on. But hell, it's not hard to cypher. We've seen men of their stripe before.

They were plenty eager to sign on for this wingding, like they had caught scent of something ripe in the bushes." Culhane looked from Chi to Cord. "They have no respect. They are flat outlaws, beyond any regard for any law of behavior, no matter."

"Like us?" Chi needled.

"No," Culhane said. "Nothing like us."

Chi studied the older man, for that answer opened up a possibility. "This business today, if there is any business: it doesn't have to be."

Culhane shook his head.

"You are letting Rawlins jerk your lines," she insisted.

Culhane stared at the tabletop. "Rawlins doesn't have much to do with it anymore," he said. He looked up to Cord. "I guess you worked out to the same conclusion."

His brows knit in thought. "There's the money. That's always part of it. Folks like us, that always has to be a part. Rawlins pledged up that twenty-five thousand, and he'll make good on it or die. I . . . someone will see to that." Culhane grinned mirthlessly. "Bounty hunting is generally outside my line, but if I kill you there is ten thousand more." He shook his head.

"But even that's not the main part. You and me, Cord, we got unfinished business that has been hanging fire too long."

"But that's not it either."

"No. There's Danny."

"You know how that was." Chi's voice had gone cold.

"I surely do. I've been dragged into that kind of thing myself, and I hold no grudge, not in any personal way. But he was my kin."

There was appeal in Culhane's tone now, as if he held their understanding in high regard. "You know how it works. Put all the rest aside and still you have got a blood reason."

Chi pushed her chair away from the table abruptly,

the sound of wood scraping wood sudden and loud in the room. Even the Reverend Paine was watching them now.

"You do what you have to," she said, and she could have been talking to either of them. "I don't guess you need my blessings."

Cord watched her go out, her Spanish spurs clanking through the stillness. When she was gone he turned back to Culhane, and the two men sat there another little spell, the talking pretty much done with.

Chapter Twelve

ACROSS THE STREET FROM THE CAFÉ A stocky black man punched a white man neatly in the mouth. It was a short punch, from the shoulder. The white man slammed back into a tethered horse, and the animal snorted and lunged sideways and whinnied, eyes wide, finally jerking its reins free. The white man stumbled to one knee and the horse reared over him, and the man tried to scramble clear and almost made it. The horse's forefoot came down on his ankle with a sickening crunch.

But Cord, watching from no more than ten yards away, could barely hear the man's agonized scream. It was swallowed in the pandemonium which possessed the town like a curse. The street was jammed with an elbowing mob of mining camp drifters, men caught up and swept on by a wave of craziness brought out by what was coming. There would be killing, right there to be watched, and the tickets drawn and paid. The word had gone out. Men on horseback in groups of two and three were riding in at either end of town.

Virtue, Cord thought sourly.

The reports of gunfire mixed with whoops and hoots and laughter. Nearly every man carried liquor or beer, and although it was barely eleven in the morning, the sun not yet full high in the hazy sky, many of the men were already stumbling and weaving on whiskey-addled legs. Near Cord a man slept in a doorway, his head wrapped in rags.

In the middle of the street a knot of four or five men in identically filthy coveralls were pushing each other around, contesting over some mindlessness, gesturing angrily with their whiskey bottles. On the boardwalk in front of the hotel a man was down on all fours, making coyote noises at the cloudless sky. An old-timer with long gray chin whiskers fired a sawed-off 10-gauge Remington shotgun into the front flap of a wall tent, a five-foot rough-edged circle of perforations emerging in the canvas when the powder smoke had cleared. A dun mustang reared loose from its hitching post at the noise of the shot and began sunfishing sideways into the street, trying to unload its saddle and stampede at the same time, until the old-timer unloosed his shotgun again. Then the horse broke hell-for-leather through the mob, scattering shouting men on either side.

Four of Rawlins's whores came out on the balcony fronting the second floor of the Gilded Palace and began screeching down to the crowd. "What you got, honey?" someone called, and a dark fat Indian woman turned and bent and threw up her petticoats to press her huge rump against the balcony rail. A bullet splintered into the building wall above her head, and she spun around to scream down a string of strange unconnected curses and swear words at the laughing men.

The crowd parted before Cord when he stepped up on the board sidewalk, and closed again when he passed. He could hear the whispering and speculating in his wake, but he had no interest in making out the words.

The saloon was even more jam-packed than the street, the miners dead-on determined to commemorate this spontaneous holiday to the hilt. At one end of the bar three of Rawlins's saloonkeeps were taking bets from the crowd. Leather pokes of gold dust were passing from hand to hand and disappearing behind the bar into a safe which stood open. A black chalkboard hung above the liquor bottles, and a man on a scaffolding was recording in four columns the amounts bet on either Cord or Culhane, and the shifting odds on each, which the man seemed to be figuring from pure caprice.

Cord couldn't help but look.

Culhane was offered at even money.

Cord was 6 to 5, against.

But that was already being erased.

Cord could not miss the comments of the bettors as he glided through the close sweat-stinking room. Four men at a table by the door were debating the chances as though they were handicapping a quarter-horse race. "They say that Cord hombre handled five men by himself yesterday."

"Shit, his wasn't the only gun that time. That high-assed Mex woman was backing him."

"You see how she done Mart Nolan?"

"That don't mean nothing. *I* could have got Mart Nolan."

"Well, you never did."

"Anyway," someone else put in, "that Cord must be some bronc-buster if he can ride her down."

"Lucky son of a bitch."

"Wonder who gets the woman if Cord gets greased."

Then there was the Culhane talk.

"You heard the stories about Texas, him riding down twelve men, picking 'em off one by one and leaving their carcasses for the turkey buzzards."

"It's there to see in his eyes, the way they're all hard, like he's always sighting in on a target."

"He's a life-taker, sure as winter."

"That's why my dust is riding on him."

"Yeah, him and his gun."

Culhane sat by the far wall, a full whiskey bottle and

an empty glass before him. Despite the press of humanity in the barroom he was alone at the table, isolated by his deadly uniqueness. He looked at Cord without the slightest sign of acknowledgment or even recognition, did not even nod.

Chi stood with her back against the far end of the bar, watching the frenzied goings-on through dark dead eyes. Like Culhane, she was apart, the miners by tacit consent allowing her a wide berth. Whether she liked it or not she had become a part of what was driving this blood-hungry mob, as if she were a prize to which these men could never aspire.

The rest of the actors were there as well: Culhane's four-man goon squad, the Kean brothers and Cooley Gaines and the breed, commanding a full center section of the bar rail and looking mostly sober and ready for business, and rather pleasured. Cord wondered which man their money backed.

Maxwell Prentiss and the Paines had staked claim to their corner table. The dime-romancer looked excited as a boy at a raree show, but the preacher had gone beyond knowing or caring. He poured the last of a pail of beer into a thick glass mug and needed both hands to get the stein to his mouth. Katherine Paine returned Cord's look with a cool appraising gaze. How far had she played her hand? Had she coppered her bet by coming to Culhane same as she had come to him? Had she gone on down the hall late in the night? But that did not matter much anymore.

"This is craziness," Chi said when Cord worked his way to stand beside her.

Cord thought she meant the gunfight, and said, "Too late now."

"All these little pig men," she said, taking in the room with a gesture, "betting on a killing. They make me sick."

"Yeah," Cord said, "but forget it. It's Culhane's doing now, agreeing to Rawlins. That's how I'm looking at it."

Chi glanced across the room to where the older gun-man sat. "I wonder how he feels, knowing all his life has come to feeding this carnival."

At the far end of the bar two men began to scuffle. The nearest bartender came around with a sawed-off broom handle and laid it across the back of one man's head. The other ducked and looked to the bartender and started to say "Thanks," when the bartender caught him over the head also, breaking the broomstick over his balding skull. The welt it left was fringed with seeping blood.

Ladd Rawlins stood on the balcony in front of his office, smiling down benignly on the crowd of men, as though all of this was his finest creation. He held up both hands in the direction of his bookmakers, palms out and fingers spread, and they began their holler to quiet the milling throng of bettors. "Ten minutes, boys. Get your dust down. The book closes in ten minutes."

Katherine Paine was pushing through the crowd to-ward them. Halfway across the room she yelped and went stiff, as if she had been goosed. She turned and slapped the nearest man across the face, so Cord reck-oned there had indeed been some unwanted familiar-ity. The man spat a curse at her, and his comrades laughed.

When she reached them Katherine was a little breath-less. There was a fine dew of perspiration on her upper lip. She looked to Chi and said, "How do you do?"

"*Hola*," Chi said without inflection.

Katherine Paine squared her shoulders, as if for an ordeal.

"Have you given it any thought?" She took Cord's hand in both of hers, letting her breast crush against his arm.

"How's that?" Cord said. She was as oblivious as the rest of them.

"You remember. What we talked about."

"What *you* talked about."

"You are deliberately trying to make this difficult for me." Katherine pouted with put-on little-girl petulance.

Cord found the depth of her self-centeredness near awesome.

"Lady," he said, "right now there is other things on my mind besides your troubles."

"You run along for now," Chi said softly. "You're making a nuisance of yourself."

Katherine looked at Chi and saw that backing off was maybe the best idea.

"*Vamonos*," Chi said.

Katherine gazed an appeal at Cord again and found in his face no support at all. She turned abruptly away, shouldering into a drunken miner and driving him into a table as she swept away.

"You know something, Mister Cord?" Chi said. "You got piss-poor taste in women. I ever tell you that before?"

"No," Cord said. "Thanks."

"Listen, *amigo*," Chi said, her voice gone gentle. "This business today . . ." She put a hand on his arm, and when he looked into her eyes he thought he saw something in them he had not noticed before, caring and concern and a look of something beyond that, close to anxiety—for him and for her as well, for their life together—whatever, it stopped Cord a moment and shook him almost physically. He wanted to say something, but no words came to mind beyond those he would never risk saying.

Up on the balcony, Ladd Rawlins began to pound on the railing with a pistol butt. The hurrahing down below subsided as the men turned to look up at him.

"The betting is closed," Rawlins announced when he had their attention. "The fight begins when the saloon is cleared."

There was a ragged cheer and men began to push toward the door. The first of them was already on the boardwalk outside, when the Reverend Zachariah Paine stood up and roared "No!"

The effect was stupefying. The sound of the single word was louder than a shotgun's boom, and the walls seemed to reverberate with its timbre. Men stood as if rooted, and the sudden silence was overwhelming.

Paine climbed onto a chair and then the table, his beer besottedness replaced by some more profound intoxication. He was hatless now, and his bristling hair stood straight on end in a swirl, streaking with sweaty gray. Cord felt a chill tickling at the base of his spine: The previous afternoon the preacher's hair had been jet black.

"Listen to me," Paine commanded, and every man in the rowdy crew obeyed. His voice rose and rolled with authority, and the men responded unconsciously like children, which most of them had been when they first heard this kind of exhortation. It still rocked them, those thundering tones.

"Ye serpents," Paine intoned. "Ye generation of vipers, how can ye hope to escape the damnation of Hell? Heed to the words of Matthew, vile creatures of the night, or forever after the inferno's fires will eat at your eternal flesh."

There was indeed something unearthly in the orotund tone of the man's voice, as if his possession were speaking with its own tongue.

"YOU!"

Paine threw out an arm, finger pointed, and every man turned to follow its direction to Cord. The great circus was beginning, and Cord stood in the center ring.

" 'Ye lust, and have not,' saith James. 'Ye kill, and desire to have, and cannot obtain; ye fight and war, yet *ye have not.*' "

Sure as he understood the man had descended into the uttermost depths of his madness, Cord was unnerved. The preacher's words scoured old sores and evoked ancient turn-in-the-night dreads. For one unmanned moment Cord was the boy he had been in east Texas, and filled with awesome frights he could not name—and still the preacher ranted on.

Paine's accusing finger swung around to his wife like an avenging sword. "And you," he thundered. " 'Upon her forehead was a name written; MYSTERY, BABY-LON THE GREAT, THE MOTHER OF HARLOTS AND ABOMINATIONS OF THE EARTH.' " His long arms encompassed everyone. " 'Come here,' commands the book of the Revelation, 'I will show unto thee the judgment of the great harlot that sitteth upon many waters; with whom the kings of the earth have committed fornication, and the inhabitants of the earth have been made drunk with the wine of her fornication.' "

Katherine must have heard this kind of thing hundreds of times before, in every town where her husband had set up to talk and rant and enchant the gold dust out of the miners. But her face was chalky with fear, and her breasts heaved with her panic, as if she expected her husband's condemnation to manifest itself at that moment, there in the saloon. The lust with which the men had once looked on her had changed to faint loathing, as if she had turned from the golden lady into a diseased hag before their eyes.

This was the power of the preacher.

And goddammit, Cord thought, this has gone far enough. He would not stand for another word, and yet he did not move.

"Murderers," Paine screamed. "Sodomites and Onanists!"

A pistol went off, very near Cord.

The explosion of sound paralyzed the room.

A man near the front of the crowd, startled near out of his jangled wits by the blast and roar and smoke of black powder, eyes wide—the man staggered sideways into the table on which Paine stood. The preacher tottered almost comically for a hesitation, and then the table went over, throwing him across two chairs with a crash of breaking wood. A long beat of silence, filled with heavy breathing, and then someone let out a hoot, and the scramble began.

The spell Paine had woven was broken.

Men fought and clamored for the doorway.

"You should have seen yourself." It was Chi, close beside Cord. She holstered her Colt and grinned. "You looked like a rube at a medicine show."

Cord blinked. She was trying to joke him out of his stupefaction, had seen the preacher's words getting to him. Cord took a deep breath and let it out. Okay. There was nothing divine about madness.

"Look there," Chi said.

At the other end of the bar, Cooley Gaines was slipping out the back door. There was no sign of the Kean boys or the breed.

A minute later the bar was mostly empty. A lone bartender was wondering if he should leave too. Katherine Paine stood a ways off down the bar, the color still washed from her face, staring at her husband, who lay in a pile of broken chairs, moaning like a whipped dog. Maxwell Prentiss was at the door, struggling to regain his smug satanic smile.

Culhane pushed back his chair and stood. He adjusted his gunbelt so it set proper on his hips. He nodded at Cord.

"Let's get this done with," Cord said.

Chapter Thirteen

THE SUN HUNG LIVID OVER THE BROWN hills, its heat sweeping the street in palpable waves. The air was so still the miners seemed to have brought the stink of the saloon out into the street with them, so the freshness was polluted by odors of smoke and whiskey and body rot. From the corral behind the saloon came the high hysterical whinnying of horses on the mill, the shrill sound cutting through the low murmur of the crowd. Almost directly overhead, but so high they were specks of darkness against the sky, a hawk rode with buzzards in lazy circles on the morning updrafts.

Someone had strung two ropes across the street about thirty paces apart to form a rough arena. On either side, miners stood in front of the buildings and tents in a line three or four deep. Rawlins's whores crowded the balcony of the Gilded Palace, and men peered down from its roof.

The crowd was finally subdued, the energy of the moment stopped up, the atmosphere tense with their anticipation. Or maybe they had finally felt twinges of shame, at least a recognition that the show they had come to jeer at and wager on involved men they could never be. Whichever, miners lowered their voices near to whispering and spoke with heads close, as if this were church. Some of the whores on the balcony had changed from their low-necked short-skirted saloon costumes to something more decorous they probably bought for the rare trip to Cheyenne or Denver. Others hid their bare shoulders under shawls in deference to the modesty the occasion now seemed to demand.

Cord pushed through the swinging doors of the Gilded Palace and stepped out onto the boardwalk. He turned to his right, his narrow bootheels hitting the planks with a hard defiant sound. At the rope he turned and stepped into the dust.

As he moved to the isolation of the center of the street, all the rest of it slipped away from him, leaving the job to be done nakedly alone. Cord smelled the fetor of the crowd and heard their low urgent mutterings, and then he smelled and heard nothing. It was as if some intangible barrier had come down over his senses, shutting him away and solitary amid this mass of people.

Cord stood with his mind emptied of all that had taken place over the last twenty-four hours, emptied even of reasons for this showdown. He did not think of Katherine Paine's compelling and mercenary seductiveness, nor her husband's lunacy and hatred. He did not think of the greedy betting miners, nor contemplated the rewards which would come if he won this battle, and the death which awaited if he failed. He surely did not envision the cheap romantic silliness Maxwell Prentiss would turn it into in the pages of one of his dime novels.

Even the distaste and sinking regret with which he had faced this fight were fled.

There was room in his mind for nothing but concentration on this task. His single-mindedness was not willed, but came to him as he focused in on this one thing he must do. All that existed was the fight.

As it had so often, it all came down to the killing.

Cord turned and saw Cash Culhane facing him from the other end of the dusty roped-in space. Cord saw Culhane set his feet maybe a foot and a half apart, his right hand away from his side, the elbow slightly crooked. Cord saw Culhane's fingers flex into a fist and come open, and then his hand hung loose, forming into the shape of a gun butt.

Cord's field of vision narrowed to enclose the man.

"Your fight." Cord's voice was heavy and dead as the air. "Make your play."

Culhane's eyes narrowed under the bent and worn brim of his Stetson, and his hand shifted so it hovered over his gun, and Cord's hand was a heartbeat away from slapping at his own weapon.

A gunshot crackled from inside the Gilded Palace.

For a moment the echo—and then on its tail the high piercing scream of a woman.

Neither Cord nor Culhane moved, did not shift their eyes from each other. The miners on either side of the street hung on the same edge of moment.

Then came the dull double-boom of a shotgun.

All hell broke loose.

One of the windows of the Gilded Palace exploded in a great shower of glass and double-ought buckshot, tearing into the men standing in front of it. Miners yowled and shrieked in pain and panic, those who had not been hit pushing and trampling over those who had gone down.

Fear and hysteria spread through the crowd like a brushfire, and even those on the edges, well away from the line of fire, began to stampede.

Three of the men who had been watching from the roof of the saloon clambered over its three-foot false front and hung a moment before dropping to the balcony. One of them landed full force on the pretty little buxom whore, and she bawled out her shock.

Then there was the wrenching sound of wood cracking and nails ripping free from boards, and the balcony, overloaded with weight and not much in the way of solid construction to begin with, tore away from the front of the saloon. It hung suspended at a radical angle for a moment before it crashed down through the canopy, shattering and splintering atop the wounded men, spilling the screeching whores into the street.

Cord and Culhane were alone in their intentions now, and still neither man had taken his eyes from the other or given up any part of his concentration to the tumult raging around him. Within a few feet, wounded men and whores lay buried and whimpering and soaked with their own blood, sobbing out for help.

"Culhane!" It was Chi's voice.

"I hear you." Still he watched Cord.

"That bunch of yours."

For several more seconds Culhane did not react. Then he frowned and muttered, "Goddamn." His right arm relaxed, and now the look he held on Cord had a question to it.

And Cord knew the moment had passed, at least for now. He searched out Chi. She had climbed over the wreckage of the balcony and was flat up against the wall of the saloon, so she could just see into the room through the hole where the window had been blasted out.

"Looks like your boys fell in with bad company," she reported.

"Let's take them." Cord spoke softly, as if he were trying the idea out.

But Culhane heard him. "Why not?"

"Let's move," Chi urged.

"You heard the lady," Culhane said. He moved toward Cord, drawing his revolver and thumbing back the hammer. Here was something for them to do together. "They would have come in from the back," Culhane said as he passed. He headed down the side of the saloon before Cord could respond.

The buxom whore lay almost at Cord's feet. On one side of her head the shiny dark hair was streaked with bright blood, a two-by-four beam pinning both of her legs. Her eyes pleaded for his help, and Cord bent and threw the board aside. Beside the girl lay a miner beyond anyone's help, a jagged sliver of glass big as a saucer sticking out from the side of his neck and all the upper half of his body covered with gore. From beneath the slant of disjointed planking which had been the balcony came the groans of others. One of the whores, miraculously unhurt, was trying to wrest loose a length of debris to get to them. She heaved and it came free, the woman's arms and trunk strong as a man's from some childhood on the plains.

Cord stepped through the bodies and litter and got himself to the side of the saloon, near to the swinging doors. He nodded a signal to Chi and spun through them at the same time she vaulted the low sill of the broken window, her Colt out before her.

The dark bearded man, the hijacker leader who had shot the freight wagon teamster the morning before when all this began, was at the bar. His left arm held Katherine Paine pinned against him, and his right held a hand gun. Katherine's head rolled like a flower with a broken stalk, though her eyes were half open. There was a blue-black bruise beginning near the point of her jawbone and reaching all the way to her left temple.

"Stop right there," the road agent leader snapped. "Don't neither of you take one more step."

What was left of the Reverend Zachariah Paine lay

in a bloody heap under the shot-out window. He had taken both barrels of the shotgun at a range of no more than ten feet. From the waist up his body was chewed raw meat. One arm was attached to the mangled torso by only a thread of sinew. The corpse was hardly recognizable as something that had been a man.

The shotgunner stood beside the bearded man. He had the weapon broken open and was seating two fresh shells in the breech.

"Drop them six-guns," the leader ordered.

"No," Chi said.

The shotgunner snapped his weapon closed and tried to fire from the hip. Chi shot him in the middle of the chest. The man rocked back against the bar and his death shudder discharged one of the loads of buckshot into the ceiling. Sawdust and splinters of wood snowed down on them.

The leader pulled Katherine Paine more erect, so his whole body was hidden by hers. He leveled his revolver on Cord and said, "That's all of it. You are finished."

"Not just yet," Cord said, and shot him in the face. The man dragged Katherine down with him as he fell, and she lay atop his body, not moving.

Chi fired behind Cord, and he whirled in time to see a man tumble from the balcony and thump on the floor nearly at his feet. From out back of the saloon came a volley of gunfire, and a moment later Culhane came through the door at the end of the bar.

"Goddamn them Kean brothers," he said through his teeth, his voice tremulous with fury. "Back-shooters put me in an awful rage."

Culhane cracked the cylinder of his Colt and upended it. Six empty shell casings slid out and clattered across the floor.

"Where are we?" Culhane said without looking up, thumbing fresh cartridges home.

"I figure the preacher drew on them," Chi said. "He was a fair hand with a gun, for all his frenzy. It looks like he got one before they unloosed with the scattergun." She pointed to where another road agent lay face down and dead, half hidden by the bar.

Cord was crouched over Katherine Paine. There was a wet smear of blood and something sticky and gray across her right cheek, but it looked to have come from the road agent leader Cord shot. She had not lost any of her own, but then her sort rarely did. Cord left her where she lay.

"That leaves one of the hijackers," he said as he rose. "Unless more came in since yesterday, and that's not real likely."

"Plus Gaines and the breed," Culhane said, nodded up at the balcony as he reseated the cylinder of his Colt. "Wait them out?"

But that question was settled before Cord or Chi could respond. They heard the door to Rawlins's office open, and the gambler appeared on the balcony, gripping the railing with two white-knuckled hands. His ruffle-front shirt was torn down the front and stained with the blood that dripped from his mouth. "Hold your fire," he wailed. "For God's sake don't shoot."

Cord caught movement from the corner of his eye, whirled and threw down in the direction of the saloon door. Rawlins yelped at the sudden movement. Maxwell Prentiss sidled into the big empty room with the stupid confidence of a man who believed himself to be essentially invisible, the perpetually uninvolved observer. There was a faint childlike smile of enchantment on the writer's face, as if this were the finest romance he could ever aspire to create, a wonderful read. He stood just inside the door, looking around the room from within the haze of his awe and delight.

The breed and the last of the road agents had come out on the balcony to stand beside Rawlins. The breed jabbed a gun into Rawlins's ribs and yanked the gambler's head back by the hair. "You heard the gambler-man. Now drop those shooters."

"Do it," Rawlins bleated. "Let them ride out, whatever they want. There's money in it for you, I swear to Christ. Do what I say."

Cord shot a look at Culhane. The old gunfighter's face was near black with rage. For a moment Cord thought the fireworks were on—and to hell with Mister Ladd Rawlins and his warped notions of money and its power.

But then Culhane chewed at his cheek, and bent and gently laid his six-gun on the floor in front of him. Cord hesitated. He had not foreseen this set-to ending in any such defeat. But in a way it was Culhane's responsibility to call the move, since it was his boys who had gone sour. Cord dropped his weapon and Chi followed his lead, liking it even less than he.

Cooley Gaines appeared on the balcony wrestling a set of saddlebags. He hoisted them over the railing and let them drop. They hit hard enough to crack floorboard.

Gaines turned his fancy dude smile on Culhane. He was having himself a time, getting the upper hand over the famous shootist. Here was a man who was known over all the West for his killer skills, mean and tough and hard-bitten, and now at the deserting gun-runner's mercy. "Pick 'em up, Culhane," Gaines ordered. "Fetch 'em outside and load 'em horseback."

Culhane said, "I will like hell," and dropped to a crouch, grappling for his Colt.

Gaines fired but the angle was all wrong, and then Culhane came up and fired seemingly without aiming. Cooley Gaines took a step back and then a step forward, his body folding and pitching over the balcony rail. Rawlins yowled in shrieking panic and twisted half free of the breed, his strength compounded by desperation. The breed fired wildly and there was a cry of pain. A part of Cord's brain registered that it had not come from Chi.

By then Cord had recovered his own Colt. He fired on the heels of Culhane, and the last of the hijackers fell back out of sight. The breed got off a second wild shot, and on the back bar a whiskey bottle exploded. Then Chi shot him.

Rawlins lowered himself to the floor of the balcony,

his hands still gripping the railing, his forehead against it, and he began to sob out his relief. Prentiss sat slumped in a chair that had escaped the shotgun blast. His right hand was pressed to his left shoulder, and he stared with bemused fascination at the blood oozing out between his fingers, as if he thought this would suddenly pass away, and things would be as they had been all along. This gunfight business had after all been his invention, and now it should be over and nothing actual—like the health of a man's shoulder—should be changed.

Out on the street a man called, "Can't move, can't feel nothing." The voice trembled with horror. "Oh, Lordy Lordy, someone help." Women, and men too, were crying.

The saddlebags which Cooley Gaines had dropped lay in the balcony's shadow. The impact had ruptured one of the seams, and gold dust leaked from it in a thin stream, like the finest of sands in an hourglass.

Katherine Paine had pushed herself into a sitting position. She rubbed at her eyes. As she looked slowly around the room, horror bloomed and swelled in her face. She touched a hand to her cheek and shuddered at the wetness there. When she saw the stain on her fingertips she began to scream, her eyes wide with terror. The eerie animal sound went on and on, until Cord finally holstered his Colt and went to her.

Chapter Fourteen

CORD PUSHED AWAY HIS BREAKFAST plate, clean except for a smear of egg yolk and bacon grease. The scrawny boy refilled their coffee cups and Cord told him to leave the pot. Cord waited while

Chi built cigarettes and then sat smoking, staring out the café window at nothing much.

After he had stubbed out the butt in his plate, Cord began to tell Chi a story in an easy toneless voice, still looking away from her. The story was about something that had happened to him years ago and long before he and Chi had hooked their traveling together. In it Cord was one of a half-dozen hands trailing a herd of three hundred beeves from near Corpus Christi up to Fort Smith in Arkansas, where the agent would distribute the animals among the tribes in the Indian Territory. The story began with a flooded river and then a stampede, and at first looked to be a sad tale about men dying young while watching over animals too stupid to know their ass-ends from their horns. But nobody died after all, and that part was just Cord's way of showing his estate in the world those days, sorely worked and coming into Fort Smith looking for high-riding ways to get shed of his sixty dollars in back pay.

"It took me maybe four hours," Cord told Chi. "I was eighteen years old and manly as all hell. First thing I did was get me a bottle of whiskey. It cost me six bits. You know the kind: flavored with a half cup of tobacco juice and a couple dashes of gunpowder. It was anyway the cheapest thing I bought that day. Well, I drank down about half of it right off, showing off to the boys that it was like mother's milk to me."

Chi grinned. Here was how it was supposed to be, as the tension of the last two days began to ease out of their systems. The two of them, together and in charge and knowing things were going to continue to work as they always had, and that was enough to make all the rest worthwhile.

Yet Cord had still felt an edge when he awoke that morning. It should not have been, and he tried to reckon what could be continuing wrong. Maybe it had to do with this no-account town called Virtue. They would be well off when they were away from it.

Drinking that much whiskey, Cord told Chi, back to his story about that time in Fort Smith, had of course put him into a blind screaming drunk inside about a half hour. The rest of his story was fitting. In a saloon, Cord said, he called for a drink "for every Texican, and every man willing to call himself a Texican," and for his trouble got beat up and thrown out by a Yankee gandy-dancer from Dover, Delaware. Not holding a grudge, Cord moved along to a poker parlor in the next joint and bet all but ten dollars of his drover pay on three kings, then realized in the showdown that one of his kings was really the jack of spades.

"I was saving that last ten dollars for something bang-up special," Cord said. Chi was laughing, and he thought how fine she looked when things were going happy. "Down near the end of Cobb Street there was a cathouse of some reputation. I went in and showed the lady my ten dollars, and she said, 'You're new around these parts, ain't you, Tex?' and I said, 'Yes, ma'am.'"

The lady had smiled real broad. "I didn't know it," Cord said, "but this was a house you only visited once. Which was its reputation. Them boys on the trail had been pulling my leg, setting me up to fun and trouble."

"Well, I went upstairs, and there was this little girl not much older than me, and she took off her blouse. I stood there staring at her with my jaw down around my belt, like I had never seen anything so fancy in my life, which was halfways right. And just then a man comes into the room, and he's got a nasty smile and a Navy Colt."

The story ended up with Cord waking sometime in the night and finding himself under a willow by the banks of the Arkansas River, all his money gone, along with his hat and boots and gunbelt. And no horse nor any idea where his horse might be, except he recalled hitching it in front of the whorehouse.

The part he remembered best to this day, Cord told Chi, was that broken-headed barefoot walk back to town as false dawn began to break, all the time thinking about the bully-ragging and hazing he would take from the men he knew awaited him in the first barroom he entered.

"They staked me to some healing-up drinks and laughed their asses off," Cord said. "And after that they called me Sundown long as I was around, because back there in Fort Smith I hadn't even made it until dark. I finally had to quit that outfit. It was the only way I could shake my nickname. They had me branded."

"Jesus, Cord." There was music and dancing in Chi's laughing voice. "You must have been some sweet hillbilly in your early days."

"That's about right," Cord said, but then the grin went away. Chi did not turn, because she had a pretty good idea what Cord was seeing.

There was something in Cash Culhane's set expression that rang a harmonic with Cord's lingering edginess, and all of a sudden he thought he knew what it had to do with. He knew Chi could feel it as well, even when Culhane came to their table and she said, "Take a seat."

"No, thank you, Miss Chi." Culhane touched fingers to his hat brim. "If you're finished up, we've got business with Rawlins. Best if we all three conducted it together."

Cord stood. If Culhane wanted this done with, it was fine with him. There wasn't much point in drawing out their stay in this hell-and-gone town.

The street was nearly empty. The few men they passed walked with heads down and eyes averted. The whole town seemed abashed, subdued, like a hungover alcoholic ashamed by the memory of the excesses of the night before, but aware he was powerless to stop himself from jumping into it all over again soon as he was well enough to hoist a glass.

This morning Virtue wanted nothing of Chi and Cord and Culhane and their ways of dealing with trouble. This day the town wanted to lie up and lick its wounds.

Someone had cleared away the rubble from in front of the Gilded Palace Casino and swept up the glass from the boardwalk. There was no sign of the dozen or so men and women who had been badly hurt, and Cord imagined them holed up in some fly-ridden infirmary tent with a broken-down surgeon, a man whose hands were so long palsied with liquor he could no longer draw patients in any town of decent folk. Cord saw the doctor picking out shotgun pellets and setting bones, and sipping from a bottle all the while. How many would lose legs or arms or lives to the mishap of wanting to see Cord and Culhane spill their blood in the street? But then, some men survived and others did not.

A line of men snaked across the barroom nearly to the swinging doors. At the line's business end Rawlins's bartenders were refunding wagers made the day before. There were no drinking customers. As each man was paid off he went quickly away, careful not to even look at the two men on whose lives he had been so eager to bet.

Ladd Rawlins stood up abruptly when Chi and Cord and Culhane pushed into his office. "Gentlemen, Miss Chi," he said, nodding vigorously, his geniality ringing as false as his tinny piano.

Katherine Paine sat in the shabby velvet-covered chair. Cord caught only a flash of the look she aimed at him; there was nothing left of her that interested him. He had known enough of her kind over the years to see from the beginning that she was not destined to play any real role in anything except his fantasies.

"You owe us, Rawlins," Culhane said flatly.

"Well, of course, I . . ."

"We did what you hired us to do, me and these folks here. Your hijackers are dead and gone to Hell, and as for your gunfight . . . well, I told you last evening." Culhane smiled a smile that was not cheering to see. "That's got nothing to do with you any longer."

"You cost me some money."

"We'll cost you some more. Twenty-five thousand, Rawlins. Each."

"Now wait a . . ."

"Don't say it," Culhane murmured, and Rawlins blanched.

"I don't have that kind of cash or dust—not anymore," the gambler said. Then he shut up again at the look on Culhane's face. "All right," he said finally. "Wait a minute."

He sat down again, bent and twirled the dial on the safe. He took out a folder, opened it on the desk, and scribbled with a fountain pen. When he was done he tore two pieces of paper from the folder and flopped them in the air to dry the ink. He handed both to Culhane.

"Those are bank drafts," Rawlins said. "Drawn against my account with the Wells Fargo Express Company and made out to 'Bearer.' They'll be honored at any bank or Wells Fargo office. I give you my word, they are as good as cash."

"If they aren't," Culhane said, "we'll be sure and let you know."

Cord took the check Culhane handed him, folded it and stuck it in his vest pocket. "That's right," he said. "And you won't like what'll happen after that."

"A moment more, please," Rawlins said, trying out a smile. "I just want to say . . ."

"No you don't," Culhane cut in. "You don't want to say a single goddamned word."

They left him sitting there, mouth agape as he studied at his check-writing book.

"How about a drink?" Chi suggested when they were downstairs. "One for the road."

"I thank you kindly," Culhane said, courtly as a duke. "But I'm riding on. There are still things need seeing to." He nodded to Cord but did not offer his hand.

Cord frowned at Culhane's back as the man walked out. The hell with it, he thought. You did what you had to, what was right, and if that was not enough it was too damned bad.

Culhane could make of it what he would, when he chose.

Cord went around the bar and took a full bottle of bourbon whiskey. One of Rawlins's bartenders looked his way and turned quickly back to his own business.

Cord started to pull the cork, then thought better of it. The liquor would go down smoother if its taste were not corrupted by Virtue's stink.

Chi was waiting for him, her gaze on the balcony. Cord looked up. Ladd Rawlins stood watching them from the height of his perch. Katherine Paine was beside him, and Rawlins's arm was around her waist, drawing her close. Both of them were smiling, as if they had won some kind of victory after all.

"Come on," Chi said, and Cord followed her out.

Old Man James, who ran the corral out back of the saloon, had saddled the bay gelding and Chi's mare and brought them around to the hitching rail. Cord gave the old man a twenty-dollar note, then waited until James had shuffled off before checking to make sure the cinches were up tight, but not too snug for traveling. The old man had managed to survive fifty years on the frontier, so Cord figured he deserved his pride.

With the bottle of bourbon stowed in his saddlebags, Cord and Chi were just making ready to mount up when Maxwell Prentiss came out of the café. He was picking the remnants of his breakfast out of his teeth with his good right hand; his left arm was suspended in a sling fashioned from a dirty gray cloth that looked to have been torn from a bedsheet. Prentiss brightened visibly when he saw them and hurried down the street in their direction. Cord had supposed that being shot might have awakened the romancer to the way of how things worked and hurt in real life, but that did not appear to be the case.

"You riding on?" Prentiss asked. When no one answered he edged a little closer, like the next part was confidential. "Say, how about you reconsider me writing up your life? I could make a name for you in the east, and you could gun for work in the wild west shows. There's the easy money. I can make you lots more famous than you are now. Or maybe you'd prefer notoriety." Prentiss waved his good hand airily. "You take your choice, famous or notorious."

"I don't think so," Cord said. He saw what Prentiss

did not: Chi was beginning to puff up with annoyance.

" 'Cord and Miss Chi,' " Prentiss proclaimed to the sky, oblivious. " 'The Robin Hood and Maid Marion of the Great West.' "

Cord sighed. Here was a man who just never learned.

Chi took one step forward and one of her high black boots flashed out. Prentiss screamed like a woman and tried to grab at his crotch with both hands, and that brought another scream as the bullet-torn muscles in his left shoulder burst into fresh pain. Prentiss fell to the boardwalk and curled up on his side, his knees drawn up to his chest and his right hand squeezed between his thighs.

Chi stood over him. "Writer-Man!"

Prentiss fought to look up at her, his fear of what would happen if he did not overcoming his pain.

"Don't you ever make us part of your lies," Chi said.

Prentiss managed to nod.

"That covers it," Cord said. "Let's ride."

They swung their horses around and headed west at a lopping dust-eating run, leaving Prentiss to gape at their backs.

Chapter Fifteen

BY THE TIME THE SUN HAD REACHED ITS apex in the southern sky they were ten miles closer to Montana Territory, and back in the clean endless wilderness. In other times this would have been enough to enliven and invigorate Cord, this wild-barren backland country. He could have quickly let go of his sour memories from the last two days. But this time Cord did not feel the peace he could usually buy from getting back into the untouched country.

Chi caught his mood and knew its source, and would leave him alone normally. But instead she had been talking since they left town, lightly teasing him, telling him made-up stories and wry fables in her idiomatic Spanish, insisting he respond in the same language.

She did not want him dwelling on the other thing. That was the way to lose it: too much thinking. That was the way a man could die. This was not over yet, and Chi knew it well as Cord.

They were coming down out of the high country now, the barren breaks giving way to the rolling hills that would fold into grassy prairie once they reached Belle Fourche, plains that stretched away to Miles City and beyond. Ahead of them the trail cut between two bosomy hills.

Cord was a length ahead when they crossed the ridge, so he was the first to see Cash Culhane, maybe fifty yards off, sitting his horse and waiting patiently. Cord reined up as Chi came alongside him. Culhane made no sign or gesture; none was needed. Cord thumped the gelding in its ribs and rode slowly forward. Chi followed.

"I reckoned you knew," Culhane said.

Cord looked away. At the foot of the rise a shallow creek meandered through a few juniper. The hills were brown this season, but come spring they would be green, and thick with wildflowers, and the creek would run high and muddy. The grass would come deep, as it always did.

Culhane had nothing new to say, but something made him go on. "You see it, don't you? It's Carson City, and my brother, and yesterday too. It's all of it."

No, Cord thought. It was none of that. It was only this: Culhane was not a man who could stand to see things go unfinished. Well, Cord thought, there is room for some of that in me as well.

"There's no talking you out of this," Chi said, but she was mostly thinking out loud. She dismounted and waited for the two men to come down on the ground with her. When they did she took the reins of all three horses and led them off toward the hills, looping the reins through the branches of a stunted juniper. There was no point in chancing them spooking and running once the shooting started. When the animals were secure, she crouched and settled on her haunches, plucked a blade of grass and began to chew at it thoughtfully, not looking toward the men.

So Cord and Cash Culhane stood facing one another in the middle of the trail with all their careful ceremony. Minutes passed and neither moved, but Cord would not be first. Even at this late moment he would not make this fight unless it was the other man's doing.

Culhane's hand moved fast as thought, and Cord's hand moved like its shadow, and the two shots were the same as they echoed over the wilderness.

Moving with great deliberateness, Culhane eased his Colt back into its holster and he nodded at Cord, took a step toward him, and another. Then he pitched forward onto the ground. It was rocky, and strewn with dead brush and dried late summer grasses.

Streaks of red streamed across the western sky. Cord patted his spade on the mound of earth, stepped back and looked it over critically, spent another moment grooming the other side before he was satisfied and stepped back.

The bottle he had taken from the Gilded Palace Casino sat beside the grave, its cork not yet pulled. Cord thought for a moment about a marker, but there was no point to that, and he anyway didn't feel up to it right then. He'd done the burying, but he would be damned if he'd read over Culhane's mortal remains.

Cord threw the spade to one side and picked up the bottle by the neck. He pulled the cork with his teeth and tipped the bottle back and let the fiery bourbon sear its way down his throat.

Then he found a place where he could sit with a tree at his back and do his drinking in comfort, as he faced the grave and the setting sun.

* * *

It had been dark maybe an hour, and Chi had not moved in that time, but went on sitting at her hideaway on the other side of the hill from Cord. Now she stood and stretched the stiffness out of her legs. A three-quarters moon splashed pale green light down around her.

She found Cord beside the grave, passed out cold as a corpse, the empty bourbon bottle a foot away where it had rolled from his outstretched hand. She stood over him awhile, and felt a wave of caring and compassion and something dangerously close to love. This was the man she had chosen to live with, and they lived in their ways. She knelt and put her hand in his, and he moaned something unintelligible and his fingers tightened around hers. She let him hold her hand for a while, realizing how hugely relieved she was that he was alive and with her.

He would not want to awaken in this place. Chi fetched the horses and walked them over, then knelt again with her canteen, slapping at Cord and splashing water into his face. He reeked of the whiskey, but Chi found the smell more reassuring than unpleasant. After a while she got him to his feet and up into his saddle, where he stayed purely by instinct and habit.

Chi fashioned loops in her riata and in Culhane's, and led Cord's gelding and Culhane's riderless animal off into the bright night. Behind her Cord sometimes moaned, and when he did she would look around to make sure he had not slipped from the saddle.

His head would hurt in the morning, but he would feel stronger the next day, and his mind would be clear. Their days together would go on as they always had. Chi headed the mare into shadowy hillsides, where the juniper floated like ghosts above the silvery cheat-grass slopes, and she whistled a sad Spanish song.

Acknowledgement

The authors acknowledge with gratitude the contribution of Jennifer O'Loughlin to this novel.

Afterword

IN *Cord: The Black Hills Duel* the character Maxwell Prentiss professes to be seeking material for dime novels. These were the grand-daddy of the paperback book, and the best-selling form of popular fiction from 1860 to around the turn of the century. The terms "dime novel" is more generic than descriptive; it refers to a soft-cover publication printed on rough pulp paper, containing a single piece of fiction of anywhere from 25,000 to 80,000 words, issued periodically and numbered serially. Depending on length, the price ranged from a nickel to twenty cents.

In 1858, Erastus Flavel Beadle and his brother Irwin P., of near Cooperstown, New York, moved to Manhattan. There, in partnership with Robert Adams, they established the publishing firm of Beadle and Adams. It first issued joke books, almanacs, "housewive's manuals," and "books of fun." Then, in June of 1860 came *Malaeska: The Indian Wife of the White Hunter*, by Ann Sophia Winterbotham Stephens, a narrative of passion and adventure owing more than a passing nod to the Leatherstocking novels of James Fenimore Cooper. It was the first of tens of thousands of entries in such series as *The Pocket Library, The Half-Dime Library, New Dime Novels,* and *Frank Starr's Ten Cent American Novels* (Starr was foreman of the Beadle and Adams press shop). *The Dime Library* alone numbered at least 1,067 titles. The early books had bright yellow covers, and were sometimes derogatorily referred to as "yellow-backs," although Erastus Beadle, who until his death in 1894 unflaggingly defended the piety and moral purity of his books, always insisted the color was salmon.

"Steam literature" (from the steam-driven printing presses used to produce it) included every popular form: romances, mysteries, and stories of war, seafaring, treasure-hunting, sports, and crime detection. One character, the detective Nick Carter, was created in 1886 and has appeared continuously since, currently in a series of paperback books, in which he has metamorphosed into a secret agent. Generally, the quality of writing in dime novels ranged from pedestrian to incomprehensible; the authors were paid as little as fifty dollars per book with no royalty participation. Yet these novels were vastly popular, not only with the juvenile audience at which they were aimed but with adults as well. It was not remarkable for a single issue to sell one-half million copies, and Beadle and Adams stories were translated into as many as eleven languages.

Many but by no means the majority of the dime novels were Westerns. Some related the highly fictionalized exploits of real figures, including Wild Bill Hickok, George Armstrong Custer, Calamity Jane (Martha Jane Canary), and Frank and Jesse James. Others about fictional characters were widely believed to concern real personalities; the most popular of these related the exploits of Deadwood Dick. Interestingly, Deadwood, like Cord, was an outlaw.

The men—and a few women—who wrote the dime novels could be as colorful as their heroes. Behind the pen name of Lt. A.K. Sims was John Harvey Whitson, who was born in a log cabin at Seymour, Indiana, in 1854 and homesteaded near Garden City, Iowa. Whitson's titles for the *Beadle Dime Library* included *Chicago Charlie, the Columbian Detective; or, The Hawks of the Lakeside League* and *Buffalo Bill at the Copper Barriers; or, Pawnee Bill's Cave of Aladdin* (the double title, with semicolon and comma, was a fixture of the dime novel). In 1898 Whitson gave up writing and was ordained a Baptist minister. The Reverend Whitson lived another thirty-eight years, during which he taught Bible history at the Ward-Belmont School for Girls in Nashville, Tennessee, and was chairman of the Religious Education Department at Hardin College in Mexico, Missouri.

Or consider Buckskin Sam, who was actually Major Sam S. Hall. A former Texas Ranger who somehow managed to fight on both sides during the Civil War, Hall curiously juxtaposed art and life by first becoming a hero in dime novels by Prentiss Ingraham, and later writing equally fanciful romances himself featuring Buffalo Bill.

But the most famous of the dime novelists was Edward Zane Carroll Judson (1823-1886), better known as Ned Buntline. The author of over two hundred books, of which perhaps thirty were Westerns, Buntline was not especially prolific by the standards of his profession. But he was a master of self-promotion, and in fact had something to promote: Buntline's own life was fully as adventuresome—and improbable—as the gaudiest dime novel. At various times sailor, mercenary soldier, blackmailer, bigamist, lecturer, political organizer, convict, actor, and murderer, Ned Buntline was also responsible for inventing the character of the man who remains today the most enduring embodiment of the Western myth.

Born in upstate New York into a middle-class family (his father eventually became an attorney), Judson ran away to sea when he was thirteen. Two years later he was instrumental in rescuing several men from a small boat which had been run down by the Fulton Street ferry in the East River. In recognition of his heroism, President Van Buren commissioned him an acting midshipman on February 10, 1838. During this service he first adopted his pen name for a series of anecdotes he published in *Knickerbocker Magazine*; a buntline is a rope at the bottom of a square sail.

For the next thirty years Buntline's life was peripatetic to say the least. In Nashville he founded a magazine, *Ned Buntline's Own*, but soon had to give it up when personal life intruded. Accused by a man named

Robert Porterfield of dallying with his wife, Buntline killed Porterfield, whose brother then shot Buntline, although not too seriously. A lynch-minded mob chased Buntline into the City Hotel. In leaping from a second-story window, Buntline sustained a leg injury which left him with a life-long limp, but he was caught anyway and hanged from an awning post. Somehow the job was botched and Buntline survived to be cut down, after which he managed to slip out of town. As far as Porterfield's original charge of trifling with his wife's affections went, it was likely true. An unrelenting ladies' man, Buntline had at least six wives in his life, several of them simultaneously.

After serving as a freebooter in the Seminole Wars, Buntline appeared in New York. There he was a ringleader of the Astor Place demonstration against German and Irish immigration; 34 people were killed and 141 wounded in the subsequent riot, and Buntline served a year and a day in the prison on Blackwell's Island for his role. Later, as an organizer for the Native American, or Know-Nothing party, he started a second riot against the German element in Saint Louis. Indicted again, Buntline skipped bail.

During the Civil War Buntline served two and a half years as a private in Company K of the First New York Mounted Rifles, but managed to avoid seeing any combat, in part because he spent a portion of his hitch in the stockade for desertion. He later claimed to have been the Union Army Chief of Indian Scouts with the rank of colonel.

After the war he toured the country as a temperance lecturer. This involved hiring a hall, printing handbills and tickets, and delivering a bombastic sermon heavily larded with cautionary anecdotes demonstrating the evils of liquor; in smaller towns it was received as a form of popular theater. Buntline prepared for each presentation with several stiff drinks.

Throughout this period Buntline wrote continually, and claimed to have made as much as $20,000 in a year from his efforts. A photograph shows him posed with a Kentucky rifle; he is wearing a serape, crossed bandoliers, bushy mustache, short-brimmed hat, and a stern manly expression.

Then, on July 24, 1869, Ned Buntline came face-up with the man he would mold into legend.

The popular version of the story goes this way: Buntline arrived by train in North Platte, Nebraska, and took a carriage to nearby Fort McPherson. There he sought out Major Frank North, commander of the post's Pawnee scouts. North had supposedly killed the Cheyenne chief, Tall Bull, in the battle of Summit Springs earlier that month, and Buntline proposed to make him the hero of a new series of dime novels he would write for the firm of Street and Smith. But North had no patience for such nonsense.

"If you want a man to fit *that* bill," he said, "he's over there."

The man he pointed out was sleeping off a hangover in a pile of straw under a buckboard. Buntline shook him awake, introduced himself, and stated his purpose. It was the beginning of a three-year relationship between the two, during which the young man would be transformed from William Frederick Cody, scout for the Fifth Cavalry, into Buffalo Bill, Western hero for all the world.

In fact the meeting was probably less dramatic. It is likely Buntline was only passing through on his way to deliver a temperance lecture at nearby Cottonwood Springs. In his first autobiography, Cody says they were introduced by Major William H. Brown. Cody describes Buntline as "a gentleman who was rather stoutly built and who wore a blue military coat, on the left breast of which were pinned about twenty gold medals and badges of secret societies. He walked a little lame . . ."

Whatever the circumstances, there is no question the two hit it off from the beginning. Although just twenty-three and half Buntline's age, Cody had a lot in common with the writer. An outgoing man with an instinctive sort of rough-hewn social grace, Cody enjoyed a good adventure in both the doing and the telling, and he shared Buntline's immoderate fondness for booze. Most significantly, Cody had already demonstrated a flair for self-promotion and judicious opportunism. Cody and Buntline were made for each other; they would become the most efficient team of publicity hounds—celebrity and agent—since Samuel Johnson and James Boswell.

Buntline spent the next week or so with Cody, riding along on a scouting expedition and listening to the young man's heroic yarns. Cody told how he rather than Frank North had killed Tall Bull (and he was probably telling the truth), and many more tales which at least flirted with the facts.

Buntline returned to New York and wrote *Buffalo Bill: King of the Border Men,* the first installment of which appeared in the December 23, 1869, issue of the *New York Weekly*. The incidents were mostly cribbed from the life of Wild Bill Hickok, and Cody is portrayed (to his own subsequent surprise) as a vociferous teetotaler. This was the first of 557 dime novels about Buffalo Bill. His public persona was invented, or at least begun.

Partially as a result of this publicity, Cody was in demand as a guide for celebrity buffalo-hunting parties. His clients included the British Earl of Dunraven, the Grand Duke Alexis of Russia, and *New York Herald* editor James Gordon Bennett. In early 1872 Bennett invited Cody to New York, paying his fare and boarding him at the Union Club. A dilettantish interest in things western, not unlike today's fad in clothing, was beginning to develop, and Bennett meant to exhibit Cody to New York society.

Although Cody possessed social confidence beyond his experience, and through his life was attracted by the regard of the rich and urbane, the whirl of New York City life got to him after a few weeks, and he looked up his old drinking pard, Ned Buntline. They had remained fond friends. In his autobiography, Cody says he considered naming his first son, born November 26, 1870, Elmo Judson Cody, in Buntline's honor.

(The boy was named Kit Carson Cody; he died at the age of five and a half from scarlet fever.)

Buntline took Cody to a performance of *Buffalo Bill: The King of the Border Men* at Niblo's Garden in the Bowery. The play was adapted by Frank C. Maeder from Buntline's novel. Cody was recognized and asked to come on stage to address the audience. Although he suffered a paralyzing attack of stage fright, the show's producer offered him $500 a week to play himself.

Cody declined, but he and Buntline saw the same light. There was money to be made from the name of Buffalo Bill. Why should it not be made by the man himself—and, of course, his creator.

During the summer and fall of 1872 Buntline sent Cody several letters urging him to play himself on the stage. Cody, aware of the money and opportunity offered, finally swallowed his apprehensions and agreed. He was to supply ten authentic Sioux and Pawnee Indians; Buntline was to write an original drama. On December 12 Cody arrived in Chicago with no Indians. But that was fair enough; Buntline had written no play.

Buntline went to his hotel and produced a script in four hours. It included a part for himself, which he padded with one of his old temperance lectures. When the curtain went up at Nixon's Amphitheater four nights later, Cody instantly forgot all his lines.

With ad-lib prompting from Buntline, he managed to get through the first act by telling some old campfire stories. In the second act Buntline's character was killed (one critic suggested the play would have benefited had he been killed in the first act, before the temperance lecture), and in the third act Cody used blanks to kill off a herd of Blue Island Avenue derelicts dressed in breech-cloths and war paint. The performance was vigorously melodramatic and outrageously overacted. The reviewer for the Chicago *Times* said of the ersatz Indians, they have a strong desire to capture somebody and, consequently, jump about and yell," and concluded, "such a combination of incongruous drama, execrable acting, renowned performers, mixed audience, intolerable stench, scalping, blood and thunder, is not likely to be vouchsafed to a city for a second time—not even Chicago." The New York *Herald,* the newspaper of Cody's one-time patron James Gordon Bennett, was less kind. It's critic wrote:

> "Mr. Judson (otherwise Buntline) represents the part [of Cale Durg] as badly as is possible for any human being to represent it. The Hon. William F. Cody, otherwise 'Buffalo Bill,' occasionally called by the refined people of the Eastern cities, 'Bison William,' is a good-looking fellow, tall and straight as an arrow, but ridiculous as an actor. Texas Jack is not quite so good-looking, not so tall, not so straight, and not so ridiculous. Ned Buntline is simply maundering imbecility."

Cody, who throughout his life enjoyed a story at his own expense, wrote later that he agreed with the critics wholeheartedly. But the ticket-buying public ate it up. Opening night grossed $2,800; later, a one-week stand in Boston was a sellout at $16,200. For the next six months the show was on tour—New York, Philadelphia, Rochester, Buffalo, Cincinnati, and Saint Louis, where Buntline was rearrested on the twenty-year-old bail-jumping rap. When the show closed at Port Jervis, New York, on June 16, 1873, Cody was $6,000 richer and infinitely wiser.

At this point Cody and Buntline parted professional company. Neither ever wrote of acrimony between them, and to contemporary witnesses the split appeared amicable. But as time passed and Cody's star ascended, Buntline the entrepreneur must have rued the break.

For the next five years Cody spent his time acting in the winter, and scouting and fighting Indians in the summers. In 1876 he was chief of scouts for Major General George Crook's Big Horn and Yellowstone Expedition against the Sioux and Cheyenne, in the aftermath of Custer's defeat. In 1883 he staged his first Wild West (Cody never used the word "Show" in the presentation's title), and from then until shortly before his death in 1917 he pursued a successful show business career. He was frightened in the end as he was at the beginning—but this time by the notion of dying in the arena, before the eyes of strangers. Ironically, Frank North, Buntline's first choice for stardom in 1869, suffered this ignominy; he died from injuries sustained while performing in Cody's show in 1885.

Would the Buffalo Bill of memory and legend have evolved had Ned Buntline never appeared on the scene? Probably. First, Cody was a legitimately heroic figure, with claims to fame as a Pony Express rider, Union soldier, scout, meat hunter, and Indian fighter, and he had the savvy to capitalize on his reputation. Most of his showman's art evolved some years after his association with Buntline, and is attributable to his own poise and self-confidence.

Second, Buntline's objective contribution was slight. It is unlikely the dime novelist either created the nickname "Buffalo Bill" or bestowed it on Cody. There were at least a half-dozen Buffalo Bills on the prairie at various times; one is mentioned in a *National Police Gazette* article published in 1846, the year Cody was born; an English tourist named Edward Shelley recorded in his journal meeting another in Fort Benton, Montana Territory, in 1862 when Cody was at least a thousand miles distant. There is circumstantial evidence that Cody himself was known by the name as early as 1867, when he first worked as a meat hunter for the Kansas Pacific Railroad; this predates his introduction to Buntline by two years.

Actually, it appears that despite Buntline's long career of promotion and hucksterism, he reached the limit of his capabilities with Cody in 1873. Don Russell, one of Cody's biographers, perceptively illuminates Buntline's inadequacies:

Ned Buntline . . . wrote the first Buffalo Bill dime novel, but he failed to make it either contemporary or western. He brought Buffalo Bill to the stage, but failed to understand the value of Cody's show-manship. Ned's translation of the dime novel to melodrama suggested a publicity device that served Cody well, but Ned failed to see its possibilities. His greatest failure, however, was in not discovering the Western; after pointing the way, he turned his back on it.

. . . By the time of his professional separation from Cody, Ned Buntline was fifty, and getting old for the adventurous life. He subsequently confined his activities to writing, the local politics of his birthplace, Stamford, New York, and the sport of fishing, in which he became an authority, contributing articles to *Forest and Stream*. His only other attempt to ally his image with that of actual Western figures came in 1875, when Buntline presented three famous peace officers—Wyatt Earp, Bat Masterson, and Bill Tilghman—with customized handguns he named Buntline Specials. Specially commissioned from Colt Firearms, these were .45 revolvers with twelve-inch barrels and "NED" engraved on the walnut butt. Masterson and Tilghman cut the barrels of their Specials down to a more practical eight inches and used them as workaday sidearms, but Earp, whose knack for self-promotion rivaled Buntline's, continued wearing his Buntline Special on ceremonial occasions well into the present century.

Buntline died at home in Stamford of heart disease. He was sixty-three years old, and had also been suffering for years from sciatica, gout, and the effects of a lifetime intimacy with hard liquor.

Dime Novels; or, Following an Old Trail in Popular Literature, by Edmund Pearson, provides an anecdotal overview of the yellow-backs. It was published in 1929 for an audience which recalled the books firsthand.

The authoritative biography of Ned Buntline is *The Great Rascal: The Life and Adventures of Ned Buntline,* by Jay Monaghan. In his Cody biography, *The Lives and Legends of Buffalo Bill,* Russell takes the view that Buntline's contribution to the Buffalo Bill legend has been overstated; John Burke takes a generally opposing stance in his biography, *Buffalo Bill: The Noblest Whiteskin*. Chapters 1 and 2 of *The End and the Myth* volume in the *Time/Life Old West* series consider dime novels and the Buntline-Cody relationship; the text is by Paul O'Neil. Cody gives his version in *The Life of Hon. William F. Cody, Known as Buffalo Bill, the Famous Hunter, Scout and Guide: An Autobiography*, published in 1879 and since reprinted. Interestingly, it has been suggested that Buntline ghostwrote this book, although that possibility is now generally discounted on the basis of textual evidence.

Two movies are of particular interest: *Buffalo Bill* (1944, directed by William Wellman) and *Buffalo Bill and the Indians, or Sitting Bull's History Lesson* (1976, Robert Altman). Ned Buntline is played by Thomas Mitchell in the first and Burt Lancaster in the second. Given Hollywood license, he is actually presented with some degree of accuracy in both.

William Kittredge
Steven M. Krauzer
Missoula, Montana
Spring, 1982

Ride into the world of adventure with Ballantine's western novels!

Ballantine brings you the best of the West— And the best western authors